SI

almost home

almost home

jessica blank

HYPERION · NEW YORK

Printed in the United States of America
First Edition
10 9 8 7 6 5 4 3 2 1
ISBN-13: 978-14231-0642-5
ISBN-10: 1-4231-0642-3
Library of Congress Cataloging-in-Publication Data on file.
This book is set in 11.4-point Janson Text.
Designed by Elizabeth H. Clark
Reinforced binding
Visit www.hyperionteens.com

For Erik

eeyore

tracy hangs out up against the fence some days, blond hair dangling down in strings toward her tattoos, dirty hoodie sticking through the chain-link holes in little bunches, her weight curving the wire till it looks like it might stay that way. Tuesdays and Fridays, after pre-algebra and lab science, she's always there: the days my backpack is the heaviest and it takes me forever to get through the parking lot and by the time I finally get to the buses I'm practically panting from trying to rush through fast enough to not get stopped by Jenny Kirchner and Julia Birmingham who corner me between the cars, throw my stuff on the pavement and call me whore. I know what Tracy's name is; I heard some seniors say it once and after that I said it over in my head so I'd remember.

Two years ago Lynnbrook Middle closed down. Sixth grade went back to elementary and they stuck seventh and eighth in with Canyon High. I cried when they sent the letter home that said my sixth-grade class was staying back. I tried not to show it but one of the tears fell down on the paper and made it rattle with this thick kind of splat so then my stepmom Linda wanted to discuss my feelings for like an hour and a half. I kept my mouth shut till she was done discussing. At the end of it she put her hand on my wrist like she was satisfied we'd had some deep communion and then I went downstairs and tried to figure out how I could get a lock and put it on my door without her noticing.

Without a car or knowing anyone who had one, I couldn't really do it. Brian turned fifteen and got his learner's right when I started sixth grade but I wasn't about to ask him. I wasn't about to even talk to him, not after he started coming in at night, creaking on the stupid beige carpet from his room next door, breathing his nasty breath on me. Sometimes I'd watch him across the table when we all sat down for dinner Linda brought home from Whole Foods, though. He'd glance up quick and look away but I kept my eyes on him and after a while he'd start to sweat into his pesto-feta pasta. Sometimes his cheeks turned red to match his zits, and for a minute I could make *him* feel things instead of the other way around. Dad and Linda never noticed but I'm still waiting for the day when they ask Brian what the matter is. I'm curious to see what he'd come up with.

The whole year of sixth grade they never asked. When Dad and Linda weren't there Brian was never nervous and he made my insides twist around like butterflies in my stomach, except their wings beat so hard I was always about to throw up.

Most of the time I just closed my eyes and kept it down by imagining things. I tried to think of places to go inside my head. I didn't believe in other lands anymore: I got sick of the unicorn stuff by the time fourth grade ended, and by sixth I was done with making Barbie living rooms, even ones with graffiti on the walls and the Barbies all in cut-up clothes and bald. So basically by then what was left to picture in my mind was seventh grade and Canyon High.

After a few months of imagining, it started seeming cooler: in my mind the lockers loomed up tall like trees making a corridor that led to an entrance to something I could never see and was always inching closer to. Once I walked through that invisible entrance I'd have a new name and face and nobody could touch me then. Maybe there'd even be kids who'd give me cigarettes behind the auditorium.

Two weeks into seventh grade, I realize that's a bunch of bullshit. There are kids who smoke on the hill behind the auditorium, but they're all a foot taller than me and never look when I walk by. I thought the whole point of being a misfit was you're always looking for the other people like you. Loneliness is like a vacuum: it's supposed to suck the other lonely people in like dust till finally it fills up and you're not lonely anymore. I try walking across the hill super slow to give them lots of chances, let them notice that I'm like them, but they never do.

The only difference between here and Lynnbrook, besides the SUVs always almost hitting you in the parking lot, is I'm that much nearer to my fucking stepbrother.

Oh, plus lockers. The whole first two weeks I never used mine because I was afraid I wouldn't know how. But after I give up on the hill behind the auditorium I start wanting someplace to go between classes so I'm not always the first one alone in the room with the teacher, and it takes a couple days to get my guts up before I finally try. I spend like five minutes trying to unlock it. I can't remember if you're supposed to go left first or right and how many times you're supposed to pass the first number on the way to the second. I try like thirty times till there's actual sweat on my forehead and it feels like everyone's staring and by the time I finally get it open the bell rings so I can't even remember which way I turned the lock. The hallway between me and English class gets emptier and it doesn't lead to anywhere besides another classroom with yellow walls and buzzing lights and posters tacked up beside the blackboard and the flag.

That night Linda starts asking how Canyon is and after that she won't stop. She wants to know my teachers' names and if I'm making friends and do I enjoy the "curriculum." Plus she starts dropping these weird phrases in, like New Experiences, or Special Feelings, which I know mean, *Are there boys I like.* One time I almost tell her she should ask her stupid son about *his* Special Feelings and try leaving me alone, but before I can say it a sick feeling comes from my stomach up into my throat and I have to bite my tongue to keep it down. A little piece of tongue comes off between my back teeth. It tastes like blood and when I go downstairs to brush my teeth it stings like crazy.

A month after school gets going Tracy starts showing up outside the fence. I know right away she doesn't go to Canyon: her clothes are way too dirty, she has these weird tattoos that look like stick drawings a little kid would make, and hardly anyone ever talks to her. If she went to school here Jenny Kirchner and Julia Birmingham would be on her all the time, not to mention their jocko boyfriends and probably even kids lower down the totem pole than that. Tracy's weirder than even the geeks and the retarded kids, with patched-together clothes that are all either black or this kind of brown that looks like it used to be white about eight years ago, her tank top worn so thin you can see her ribs through it. Her hair hangs all stringy in her eyes, and not like she put Molding Mud in to look like Jennifer Aniston at the Oscars when I was eight but like she never washes it, and bleached so yellow that it's almost green. If she went to Canyon she'd be getting her ass kicked every day, backpack torn off her shoulders and thrown into her face and fuck it if the books are so heavy they bruise her. But she's just alone. A couple times goth kids with black mesh shirts and wallet chains hanging from their weird huge pants go up to her, and one time this junior guy who Brian knows from soccer starts talking to her and then stops when a bunch of seniors walk by. Besides that she just leans back against the chain-link, her back to the blacktop, and watches everyone. When teachers come out to their cars she stands up straight and goes near other kids, trying to look like she's part of their after-school clumps; once the grown-ups are gone she just glares at the kids and goes back to the fence.

Dad and Linda are proud of our house. It's up in Beachwood Canyon, tucked behind Hollywood, and the streets snap around the sides of the hills and everything is green. When we first moved in five years ago my dad taught me the names of almost all the flowers in the neighborhood, jasmine and agave and bougainvillea; we would hike up the hills, me on my little legs, and I'd point them out, repeat back what he taught me. When we got to the top the city spread out below us big as a whole country, lavender smog cloaking the whole thing like a blanket you could see through.

I was seven then and it was me and Dad plus Linda; Brian still lived in San Diego with his real dad and I'd only ever met him at the wedding. He moved in two years later, though, when something happened to him down in San

Valley Camp ones. "Eleanor," my dad said which he only calls me when he thinks he knows more about something than I do, "you can't just throw out all your clothes. It's wasteful." Whenever I don't agree with him about something he always makes me describe what he calls my Reasoning. He started doing it at the end of sixth grade, all official like it was some kind of special grown-up thing but I wasn't about to tell him my "reasoning" for throwing out my T-shirts so I just said "Fuck you," but too soft for him to hear. Linda came in from the hallway and stood in the door and gave my dad this smirk I wasn't supposed to see, like she knew the magic answer and it was a secret, and then my dad turned red and Linda took me on a special trip to the mall the next day. She wanted to take me to Nordstrom and talk about outfits. Instead we went to Foot Locker and I bought four hoodies, size XL, red, navy, black, and gray, and then we had Sbarro, and then we went home.

And yet. Matt Ditkus and Marco Rollo start it in second-period English the first Tuesday in October with some shit they drew on graph paper: this girl with hair down to her chin like mine and a double-pierced ear which I also have, except her body is all bikini-looking like a *Maxim* cover and she's about to fall over from her boobs being so big. But it says "Elly" on the bottom so I know it's supposed to be me. Matt Ditkus throws a wad of paper at my back halfway through the period and when I turn around he holds the drawing up. Which of course everybody sees.

After that you can hear like five of them back there the rest of the period cracking up and when the bell rings my new nickname is Tits.

Brian heard my nickname in the halls, I guess, because he tries calling me it at home the next night. I wish I had a pencil I could stab him in the eye with so it'd spurt blood and make him blind forever, but instead I just keep watching *Total Request Live*. He laughs and then calls me it again before he goes downstairs. I can't go down there after that so I try to stay upstairs on the couch till I fall asleep and it works for a while, through back-to-back *TRL*s and *Road Rules* and some thing with Seann William Scott. My eyes are starting to droop half the time and I know if I can get through one more hour of videos I'll be home free, upstairs for the night in the living room with no doors for Brian to close behind us.

But then of course Linda comes home, thinking she can just breeze in after working till practically midnight and start rearranging everybody. My dad went to bed like four hours ago for a morning meeting; even if I never get to see him, he at least lets me sleep where I want. But Linda wiggles my shoulder saying "Baby, wake up, you won't get a good night's sleep on the couch," and I want to tell her I was getting a perfectly good night's sleep before she fucking woke me up, but instead I just sort of mumble and try to sound as asleep as I possibly can, hoping she'll give up.

There is nothing more annoying than the exact sound of Linda's voice when she is saying my name to try and wake me up. And of course she keeps doing it so eventually it becomes so incredibly irritating that I am forced to open my eyes. "Yeah?" I say, making my voice all bleary.

"Come on, sweetie, time to go downstairs," she says, and there is no way to explain that the idea of going downstairs makes me feel the kind of panicked dirty that happens when you go without a shower for so many days that the grease on your face starts making you itch so I just say "Okay," and take the steps as slowly as I can.

The Ashlee girls love Matt and Marco and their JV friends; they all hang around the double doors at lunch looking like some Abercrombie ad and start giggling like little screechy birds when the guys come out from the cafeteria. The week after Matt Ditkus dubs me Tits I'm sitting on the sidewalk across from the double doors eating Tater Tots when Marco sneaks up to the cluster of girls from behind. He puts one arm around Jenny Kirchner's neck and feels her up with the other hand. She makes this weird noise, sort of halfway between a scream and a laugh except both. The other girls keep bird-giggling, but louder like a swarm. Jenny's smiling when she throws her head backward onto Marco's shoulder, except she doesn't really look like she's breathing. Her stomach is sucked in so much you can see the lines of the muscles like a magazine girl, and her hair falls off her thrown-back neck like she's waiting for Dracula. She is perfect: every part of her fits together just the way it is supposed to and even though my chest feels weirdly tight I just want to watch her forever. I wish I could be invisible and frozen, just so I could stay here looking. Then Matt Ditkus turns around and sees me. "Tits!" he yells and my stomach fills up with spastic butterflies and my face gets so hot it starts sweating and I know it's red. I hate him. There's nothing to say though and I'm done with my Tater Tots so I just look down at the asphalt like it's the ceiling and memorize it till he turns his back on me again.

The next time I see Jenny Kirchner after that, in B hall before lab science, she makes this gross-out face, then leans in to the other Ashlees and starts whispering at exactly the amount of loudness that I can tell it's about me but exactly the amount of quietness that I can't hear what it is. For I don't know what reason the feeling I get makes me think of Brian and the spastic butterflies start again. It's retarded that I'm embarrassed by the Ashlees whispering when I don't even know what they're saying; usually I just hate them, but somehow Matt Ditkus seeing me see Jenny made the whole thing different, not to mention that he and Marco have now taken to calling me Lesbo in addition to Tits. When the bell rings Jenny goes "So we'll see you after seventh period, right? Bye!!" like she's inviting me to the mall with them but I know that isn't what she's doing.

If they were just going to throw my stuff on the ground again I don't know why she'd make such a thing about it. They've got some kind of other idea I'm sure and all through lab science I watch the clock, willing the seconds to stretch out like rubber bands, each one pulled out three times its length and so, so skinny. Eventually they hit their limit and the bell rings, making my face sting like a thousand rubber bands snapped back all at once, and I almost cry.

In the parking lot, Jenny Kirchner has a plan. She and Julia and the Ashlees are standing halfway to the buses in a cluster; they're watching the doors when I come out, and I can tell they've been waiting. I stalled in the girls' bathroom for fifteen minutes after last bell, hoping I would miss them. Everyone else is loaded on the bus, doors closed, but they're still here. The weird thing is no backpacks. They've got their hands free and I wonder where their stuff went till I see the JV guys off to the side, laughing in their baggy shirts and shoving each other, the girls' matching backpacks piled at their feet. It's the guys' job to stand near them because the girls all have another job; I know it even though I don't know what it is.

There's no other option but to walk right toward them. If I walked back into the building it would mark me for life. It's one of those face-off things, like *West Side Story* or some cowboy movie. You can't turn around; they'd just shoot you in the back anyway. So I keep going, even though the sweat from my armpits is cutting cold trails all the way down to the waist of my jeans and my ears are burning up. I figure I'll just watch the asphalt till they're done calling me whatever names and then they'll let me go.

When I'm ten feet away, Julia Birmingham starts walking toward me. She looks like Brian when he's playing soccer, eyes fixed on me like I'm the ball and the team'll lose if she doesn't kick me hard enough. Behind her is this curly red-haired girl whose name I don't know; she's stocky like me but stronger and I wonder why she's there with Julia like some bodyguard. Then Julia makes a run and before I can even look up she's got the bottom of my hoodie in her fists and she's pulling up, so hard I have to lift my arms or it feels like they'd break, and then some other girl's unbuckling my belt and I almost need to pee. I wiggle around like a goldfish spilled from a Baggie but it's just as pointless as the fish because then they're all on top of me, ripping at my clothes from ten directions and I try to keep my eyes on the asphalt but there's just no way because their hands are in my face every five seconds. I think they're all about to hit me but they don't, they just keep tearing at my clothes till all that's left on top is my ugly fucking grandma bra, and that's half gone too; my jeans are down around my ankles and the rest of my clothes torn up. I can see out the corner of my eye that Jenny Kirchner is just standing there with her arms crossed, untouched and smiling, like she's the fucking queen of everything and didn't even break a nail. I feel a hundred pairs of eyes on me as I hear the buses shift into gear to leave.

I try to bend over, grab my waist and curl around it, not caring that they might jump on me again; but Julia and the redhead grab my wrists and stand me up, hold my arms behind my back so hard it feels like my shoulder blades overlap, and they turn me toward Mike and Marco and the guys. The guys are laughing, hitting each other and staring at me; I can't even tell what they're yelling. About a thousand different things. The snot is salty in my mouth, my neck and chin sticky with tears. I feel like a dog pinned to the ground by a pack of bigger ones, my stomach fat and naked, like all they'd have to do is dig in and I'd be dead.

But then the fingernails pull out of my skin and the knuckles loosen around my wrists and the laughing gets quieter, like a car stereo driving away, and I crumple down to the ground and no one stops me. When I open my eyes the girls are all clustered up by the guys, picking up their backpacks, backs to me. I wait to look at them till I can tell from the corners of my eyes that they're headed somewhere else, and I wait to pull my clothes on till they're closer to the somewhere else than they are to me.

The lot's almost empty, except a couple seniors smoking by their cars and the after-school monitor, whistle around her neck like a gym teacher, so far on the other side of the lot that she's just a little pinprick dot. Linda always says to call her if I miss the bus, but I'm sure she's In a Meeting and if she's not her first question will be what I did to be so late and I am not ever ever telling her why I missed the bus today, not ever. I'm thinking about walking, even though I'm about to puke and my eyes are so bloodshot the veins in them actually hurt, when I feel someone standing there again. I pull my breath in and hold it, ready for Julia or Jenny or the redhead, but then nothing happens so I look up. It's Tracy.

"Come on," she says. "I'm not supposed to be on school property." I don't know what she's talking about but somehow I know if I do what she says it'll be better.

I wipe the snot off from above my mouth and then go for my eyes. I don't know what Tracy saw and what she didn't so if there's any way I can look like less of a pathetic dork I'm gonna try. But then she says "Come *on*" again like she thinks it's way more lame that I'm wiping my face off than she does that I was crying. I leave the rest of the wet on my face. When I stand up I get a head rush and my stomach flops over inside and everything goes spotty and black. Before I even realize I'm about to fall down I think: shit I can't fall on my ass in front of Tracy, and get this panicky feeling like right before Julia started running toward me. But Tracy just grabs my arm and even though I practically weigh twice as much as her she holds me up, even when I get dizzy again and lean all the way into her hand.

Then the head rush goes away and I stand up straight

but Tracy's still holding on to my arm. Her fingers feel like they're made only out of bones with no skin or anything around them but somehow they're strong. She pulls on me and starts walking and I follow.

Once we're off the parking lot and across the street she turns to me. She's four or five years older, Brian's age, but also there's this other thing I don't know what it is that makes her look really old, like forty, which I've never seen before. Up close I can see her zits and the circles under her eyes which are really more like shadows and her eyes are the color of ice. Then she says "Are you okay?" to me and the look she has is the look that Linda's always trying to fake when she asks me how school was but I can tell Tracy actually wants to know the answer.

"Yeah, I'm okay," I say but I can't look at her and talk at the same time. I try to wipe some more snot off so she won't see. By now what's left is crusty.

"Those kids are fuckin' assholes," she says to me.

"Yeah, whatever, I know." Still trying to get the crust off.

"No, those kids are fucking assholes. They're *shit*." She says it like it's really important that I understand; it kind of scares me. I look up at her. "Those kids are little shits, they don't fucking know about anything and they'll do that to people the rest of their lives because they're fucking weak. You can't let them make you fucking cry."

She has this look in her eyes like a really sharp knife

and all I can say is "Okay." It comes out really quiet.

"What?" she says, all pissed.

 I can't tell if I said the wrong thing or I just said it too soft but I have to answer so I say "Okay" again, louder. I look at her eyes after. For practically thirty seconds she just watches me and I know I'm not supposed to look away so I don't.

Finally she goes "All right" and stops seeming mad. "They're assholes, okay?"

"Okay," I say again, but I breathe first and look at her when I say it this time, and she looks at me back. She's beautiful. I can't really explain it since she has a face full of zits and her teeth are yellow like her hair and she looks like she hasn't slept or showered in a week or eaten in a month. It's not anything about the pieces of her fitting together right like Jenny Kirchner or matching up with anything I've seen before. It's more about how Tracy's got all this metal in her eyes like she knows five million things I've never even heard of, but then she looks at me like I know all those things too.

 I still can't look at her, though, because I don't know what's supposed to happen next. I can't get home unless I call Linda or walk, which'll take at least an hour. And the idea of showing up two hours late, all bloodshot with my clothes ripped up, and getting the third degree is worse than what already happened. Not to even mention Brian. Who probably saw the whole thing. And when I realize that I actually almost throw up.

"Wanna go get a taco?" Tracy asks me.

I follow her all the way under the 101 and down to Sunset.

The place on Sunset has some guy she doesn't want to see, she says when we're close enough to know, so she tells me keep going down to Benito's on Santa Monica. When she says that I get a kind of flutter in my throat: Linda and I pass Benito's sometimes on the way to the highway and there are always transvestites there, and I'm pretty sure they're hookers. They're tall and loud with big lips and leopard print and faces that look more like billboards than like either a man or a woman. On the way to Route 10 I always watch them out the window without letting Linda see my eyes.

I'm kind of nervous to be near them and I wonder if Tracy knows that they hang out there. She doesn't look nervous so I think she must not know. When we get close up their makeup is so thick you can't see skin underneath but you can tell that it's bumpy. They have long fake eyelashes and little red purses and their lip liner is perfect. One of them has a Spanish accent; I try to eavesdrop but Tracy interrupts. "Do you have five dollars? I'm out," she says, and I've got some allowance left over so I buy her two chicken tacos and a large horchata. My stomach doesn't feel great but I get a taco anyway: I know I always feel dumb when I'm the only one eating and I don't want to make her feel bad.

We sit on the stools while we're waiting for the food; Tracy spins hers around and I watch the big slabs of meat sizzle on the grill. I've never gotten food someplace with anyone besides my dad or Linda. Jenny and Julia and the JV guys all go to In-N-Out Burger when they get a ride from someone's older brother, or the food court at Hollywood and Highland, but I never have. It's a whole different thing, being able to get whatever you want and having someone to eat it with too. I could have a large Coke for dinner or just some chips, and nobody's going to tell me to watch my nutrition.

I feel like a grown-up next to Tracy waiting for our food. Or not like a grown-up really, but something different from a kid. I feel like if someone saw me they would think that I looked cool. I've only ever thought that about other people. But now I think that I could lean against the counter and look just like a picture. I try it: lift my chin up, sort of squint my eyes. Tracy spins a half-circle toward me. "What are you doing?" she says. "You look fuckin' weird."

My face gets hot and I know it's red which makes it hotter. "Who're you making that face for, anyway?" she asks me. I don't want to tell her the answer, which is her.

Just then our food comes up and I'm totally relieved: I can change my face without looking like I'm doing it on purpose. Tracy tears up the tinfoil around her tacos; the way she eats them reminds me of a dog who just got people food. "What's your name?" she asks when she's done swallowing.

It's weird she doesn't know since I know hers, but I guess why would she. I tell her and she scrunches up her nose. "That's not your name," she says and I wonder if she heard people call me Tits and that's what she means. I can't ask her though so I just sit there and chew. "Who gave you that name? Your parents?" and I nod through the taco. "Yeah," she says. "That's why you need a new one."

I never thought you could just change your name. Just decide it was something else and make it that. Names were something that you came with; they got decided somewhere way before you and then were part of you just like your skin or face. But Tracy goes "So what'll it be?" and looks at me and I know I have to pick and once I do she'll call me it and even if she's the only one I won't be exactly Elly anymore. I think: Amy Stacy Sarah Laura Beth but all of them are weird and sound like dolls. "Does it have to be a girl's name?" I ask.

"Fuck no," Tracy snorts. "Who told you that? Pick a word or something," but then there are so many words, and I can't think of any except Taco or Pepsi, which are both retarded. She breathes out like I'm stupid. "Fine," she goes finally. "What's your favorite cartoon?" and my life fucking sucks because the true answer is Winnie the Pooh. And if she makes my name Pooh I'd honestly rather be Tits. But I have this feeling with Tracy that if I hide anything she'll see right through to where it is, so I tell her.

She spins her stool around again and thinks and when

she comes back around to face me she says "Eeyore," and then stands up, and that's my name. The Spanish one of the transvestite hookers watches Tracy pick my backpack up and sling it on her back. I can tell she's still watching when Tracy grabs my arm and pulls me down the sidewalk; I want to look back but I don't.

By now the sun is setting and the sky is orange and I'm starting to get kind of scared. You can see the hills from where we are, and the lights in the windows all gold-colored like polka dots in the dark green of the trees. I think about Whole Foods, prepackaged pesto pasta and the dinner table, and wonder if my dad has made a phone call to school or if he's even home. Linda must be freaking out. That part makes me happy.

Tracy asked if I had enough to buy us donuts in the morning but she hasn't invited me to spend the night, which is weird. We keep going toward West Hollywood so I think that must be where she lives but she hasn't mentioned it and I don't know what I'm supposed to ask and what I'm not. Also I would think she'd have her license since she looks at least as old as Brian but we just keep walking everywhere and my feet are starting to get blisters on the bottoms.

Finally when the sky starts to turn from pink to blue I ask her where we're going. It comes out sort of mousey-sounding and right away I wish I hadn't asked but it's too late, she's already answering. "This guy I know over by

Fairfax. Probably we can crash there, plus Whole Foods throws the bread out when they close at nine."

"Aren't we going home?" I ask her. She looks at me like I just talked to her in Japanese.

"Home?" she goes. "What do you mean 'home'?" She pronounces the word like Linda says "curriculum," like it's separate from all other words and special.

"Aren't we going to your house?" I say and right away I can tell it's the wrong question. She looks at me like she looked at Jenny and the JV guys and the sidewalk sort of moves under my feet.

"You want to hang out with me or not?" she asks and of course I tell her yes, which is the absolute truth, her yellow hair is beautiful and the way she scares me is brand new and so much better than how Brian does or the idea of going home so late, having to see his face after he probably saw me naked in the parking lot. "Okay, then," she says. "We can probably crash with this guy. Otherwise it's warm behind Whole Foods and they almost never bust you."

The bottom of my stomach feels like at the top of the first hill of the roller coaster just before you tip and go down: wanting to get out but knowing there's no way so it just fills you up till you can feel all your veins and your blood and your insides lift up like something is about to happen and you just hope the bar over your lap holds. Tracy is talking about sleeping outside. I would never be allowed to do this, no way not ever. Sometimes Brian stays out past midnight but they always know where he is, and this isn't one in the morning it's all night; it's not some soccer team kegger, it's outdoors. I never even heard of sleeping outdoors besides camp. And this is not camp, it's Hollywood. Somewhere underneath the feeling in all of my skin and stomach and veins I can tell that for about one more minute I could decide to go home, and I'd probably get yelled at but I'd be inside my house where it's warm. But then I think about Brian maybe seeing me in the parking lot trying to cover up, him hearing everybody laugh, and somehow that makes him coming in at night not just a secret, now they all can see it, all those people sitting on the bus and watching me, their eyes are all so big and I am little like an ugly dirty bug. And then Tracy turns around and looks at me and makes all their eyes shrink down to tiny because when Tracy looks at me she sees an entire different thing. "Okay," I say, and hurry to catch up.

The next morning before sunrise the sky turns the color of jeans; the light wakes me up before the traffic starts. It's quiet back here by the Dumpster and the gravel in my back reminds me of the feeling of pebbles on a camping trip, except I don't have a sleeping bag, just a T-shirt Tracy gave me. Her friend wasn't home last night even when we came back to knock four times so we wound up here behind Whole Foods. I thought it'd take me forever to get to sleep but when I looked over and saw Tracy's eyes still open, watching the alley around us, I must've stopped being scared because I don't remember anything after that.

Now it's the other way around: my eyes are open, she's still sleeping. It's cold so I take her T-shirt from under my head and put it over me, trying not to make any noise. When Tracy's awake I can't watch her the way that I want to: I know she'd catch me. But now she's sleeping so hard it barely seems like she's breathing and I put my eyes on her and it feels like a kind of rest, like if I wanted to I could drink in some of her and make it part of me.

It seems like forever that I lie there watching her eyeballs twitch from dreaming and her eyelashes move against her cheek. I think this is what dawn is, the part right before sunrise when the sky isn't black but it isn't blue yet and it isn't orange either. After a while the cars start getting louder and the sky gets brighter too; it happens slow so I have a chance to get used to the idea that a day is going to start. In my head I say good-bye to Tracy sleeping and the dawn and the quiet, and then I hear myself and realize what a loser I must be.

And then I remember it's a school day. Which makes me realize last night was a school night, which makes me realize I never went home. And then my heart starts beating in my ears because what am I supposed to do? If I go home I'll get killed and I'm sure Linda's called the school by now which means the second I show up there they'll call her in and then I'll get killed too. I guess last night I just assumed

I'd be in homeroom in the morning because that's what happens every day but now I start thinking what kind of shit I'll be in if I go back there, not to mention everyone will know what happened in the parking lot and my hoodie is still ripped. Not to mention Brian. And I start realizing that maybe I can't go back to school today.

Except you can't just not go to school. You get expelled, or else in such huge trouble I can't even picture what it's like. I start really wanting Tracy to wake up.

There's sweat trickling down my sides from my armpits making me colder and my palms are all sticky but I tell myself Tracy will know what I should do and it calms me down a little. I roll onto my back and watch the sky, waiting. I count my breaths which almost always makes the time go faster; I know that from Brian.

Finally after at least three people have come around to throw stuff in the Dumpster and almost seen us, Tracy opens her eyes. She sits up and then turns to me and says "Oh yeah," like she forgot I was there. I have all these questions I want to ask right away but Linda always bites my head off if I talk too much before she's had her coffee and I think Tracy might be the same. Yesterday Tracy asked if I'd buy her donuts in the morning so I owe her; I'm hoping on the way she'll say what I'm supposed to do before I have to ask.

The whole way to Winchell's she doesn't even talk except to ask me for five bucks to buy us breakfast. At the counter she leans forward on the white Formica and smiles at the guy, who doesn't speak much English. She orders half a dozen, half jelly half glazed, and a coffee with four sugars and as he's almost finished getting them she says "How about a discount" and sort of tilts her head. What's weird is she kind of reminds me of Jenny Kirchner when she does that, but then the guy gives Tracy the donuts for only a dollar and she stuffs her pocket with the change, takes the bag and turns around and looks like herself again.

When we're back out on the sidewalk she hands me a jelly donut and goes "So how does it feel to be playing hooky?" and grins at me totally different than the smile she gave the donut guy, showing all her ugly teeth. Inside the donut is raspberry and as soon as I swallow I say "Pretty good, I guess," and that's all we ever say about it.

After that she takes me to Rite Aid. On the way in she puts her hand on my back and pushes me in front of her. I don't know where she wants me to go or what we're even in here for, but she leans in over my shoulder and smiles and I can feel her breath on my face as she pushes me forward.

The lights are bright and there's almost no one in the aisles, just bottles of things lined up and stacked to the ceiling. She pokes me in the back to point us toward the hair-dye section, where the boxes are white and all have girls on them that look the same except for different shades of hair. I wonder if they dye each girl's hair with the actual stuff that's in the box or if it's just an imitation. Tracy wanders up the aisle a little with her hands out of her pockets and I stay where I am, reading the words *Herbal Essences* over and over till the H and the E look weird. Then Tracy comes back and stands really close to me and I feel a weight in my front hoodie pocket; when I turn around she looks at me hard. She goes "I'm thirsty, let's go get some water" and then starts walking. All I know is I probably shouldn't drop anything so I keep my hands cupped below my stomach.

Tracy gets the biggest size of Poland Spring from the refrigerator case and then heads toward the front. I follow her and my heart is beating again because she hasn't told me to take the stuff out of my hoodie and we're about to get to the register. When we're there she still doesn't say anything; I read the whole front of *People* about Drew Barrymore's amazing new weight loss and move on to *In Style* while Tracy buys the water.

The register ka-chings and the lady goes "Have a nice day" in the boredest voice ever and Tracy takes the water jug and starts walking toward the door, which is a long way away. On the way there my heart weirdly slows down and I realize Tracy's never messed up since I've known her. Maybe she just knows some stuff I don't, I think, and all of a sudden that weird blurry nervous feeling goes away and it's like I just leaned back in a big soft chair except I'm still moving. My breathing sinks down into my stomach as the automatic doors slide open and Tracy and I walk right through.

As soon as we're away from the Rite Aid, the laughing

starts. It all comes out in an explosive burst and then keeps itself going in my head and mouth and it feels so good I don't want it to stop. Tracy kind of smirks at me. "Not bad," she goes and then she reaches into my pocket and pulls out what she put in there. She holds up a blue plastic box with no pictures on it that says *Lightening Power*; in the other hand she has a box of Afro Sheen hair dye on it with a black lady's picture that looks like it's really old, like from the '80s. Her bangs are kind of sculpted into curves and her hair is magenta. "I thought this color would look good on you," Tracy says, and I start laughing again.

We run around the corner to a Laundromat that's about from 1950; nobody's in it except for an old guy sleeping in one of the yellow plastic chairs. We both sit down on the sidewalk in front of it and Tracy starts ripping open the Lightening Power package. There's a piece of paper inside with teeny tiny directions. Tracy turns the box over and pulls two plastic gloves off the back and puts them on, and then she opens the blue box and mixes a powder into a little bottle that came inside. She says "Close your eyes" and squirts the bottle all over my head. It smells like floor chemicals and my scalp feels cold and then starts stinging but I stay there with my eyes closed while Tracy covers my head with the bleach. She says "Sit there for a while" and the sting turns to burning and my eyes feel hot, but then I remember how I felt on the way out of Rite Aid and it almost makes me laugh again.

After about forever Tracy goes "Okay" and tells me to bend over forward and keep my eyes shut tight. She rinses the bleach out with the water jug she bought, running her fingers through my hair; her plastic gloves on my scalp come in where the burn was. When she's done she dries me off with the bottom of her T-shirt and says "Open your eyes and stand up." In the reflection of the Laundromat window my hair is yellow just like hers.

I feel like a kid in a Halloween wig, but then I touch my hair and it's mine. Tracy starts opening the Afro Sheen package with the magenta dye and I almost stop her. I kind of want to stay blond. But the reason why is so we'll have the same color hair and I know how dumb that is so I don't say anything, I just keep looking at myself in the window for as long as I can.

After that I have purple hair. I look awesome. It makes me feel like one of the JV guys walking down the street, or even bigger, and I stick out my chest and sway my shoulders like a football player when I walk and this time Tracy doesn't say I look stupid. Every time we pass a window I stare at myself: my eyes lock on my reflection like they locked on Jenny Kirchner that day she looked so perfect and I can't stop watching the girl I see, except now she's me.

Tracy and I spend a bunch more nights outside by Whole Foods; it gets easier and easier to sleep through rush hour and the third or fourth morning I realize I sleep better out here than at home because there's no door for Brian to open halfway through the night. There's only Tracy, and as long as I'm next to her I'm safe.

After about a week my allowance runs out. I get twenty-five a week for cleaning my room and we've made it last pretty good: Tracy taught me how to Dumpster-dive plus she's really good at that trick with the donut guy so he gives us lots of stuff cheap. Once a day we get tacos or something else salty and the rest of the time it's apple fritters, day-old glazed or whatever we can Dumpster. But then one morning I reach for the wad of ones and fives in my pocket and it's not a wad anymore, it's just a dollar. I'm not sure how to tell Tracy; I'm a little afraid she'll get mad.

She takes care of everything except for money; that's my job. Once she pulled a hair band out of her pocket and I saw a little corner of green come out too but she stuffed it back down fast and didn't mention it. The next time we went for donuts I waited for a second to see if she'd pull it out but she didn't. It was fine with me.

But now I'm almost out and it's only morning and I'm not sure what we're supposed to do. I want to tell her before breakfast so she can plan ahead: I wait till she rubs her eyes and spits and sits up and then I say "Um, Tracy?" and she says "Yeah?" and I tell her. My heart is beating super fast like I did something wrong and I'm about to get caught. She doesn't look at me or talk, which makes it beat faster because I can't tell if she hates me now or not. After a long long time she turns to me and says "Okay. So where's your house?"

We wait until the clock at Winchell's says ten because some days my dad goes in late to work, and then start walking up toward Beachwood Canyon. Of course it sounds easy: I know where the key is under the fake plastic rock by the doormat, and I know where the food is in the pantry, and I know where Linda keeps spare twenties in her bra drawer and that she won't miss a few. But as the hill starts getting steeper and we get closer to the 101 I'm feeling more and more like throwing up.

Tracy can tell, I guess, because under the highway she turns to me and says "You're fucking green. What's wrong with you?" I chew on my tongue. Number one, I'm scared of getting caught, which I obviously can't tell Tracy. But more than that I'm scared of being in the house, by Brian's room, the walls and the doors and the carpet and who I am inside them clamping down around me like a snake and squeezing tight. This past week has turned me different: now I'm a girl I like to watch in windows, purple-haired and dirty, and from the way that Tracy looks at me, I can tell I know so many more things than they would ever let me. But I feel like as soon as I'm in that house I'll go back to how I was before, even if nobody's home. I don't know how to explain it to Tracy: I'm sure she's never felt anything remotely that dumb. But she just keeps staring at me, and then goes *"What?"* and I know I have to answer.

I can't let her think I'm backing out of going. The money is my one and only job; I can't not come through. If I try to explain that I'm scared the walls and carpet in my house will turn me into someone else, she'll look at me hard and like a stranger, the way she did that first night when I asked her if we were going home. Just imagining it makes me want to die. But she's making me talk so I have to say something, and for some weird reason the only thing I can figure out to explain to her is Brian.

I have never breathed a word of him to anyone and the words feel bizarre in my mouth: they've been coiled up somewhere so much farther down than that forever and now they're stretching out and up and I can feel them behind my teeth and it surprises me, like some weird food I've never tasted. I have no idea why I'm telling Tracy this or why I'd even think she'd understand. But for some reason I'm not scared. And after I get the first few sentences out from my mouth into the air she looks over at me with this kind of recognition I've never seen before in anyone, and she says "I know" and takes my hand. She holds it all the way to my house and she doesn't let me go, even when my palm starts sweating.

At the house we take showers first. I stand guard for her outside of Dad and Linda's bathroom and when she's finally done and the mirrors are all steamy, we trade off. In the shower I can't hear anything besides the water and it kind of freaks me out: I imagine someone showing up and seeing Tracy sitting on their bed; they'd call the cops. But the shower feels so good cutting through a week of dirt and grease that soon I mostly don't think of anything but that.

When I come out of the bathroom Tracy isn't there. For a second I freeze and listen: if someone came home there'd be voices. I think about crawling out the window if I need to. But all I hear is Tracy walking around below me. I call out her name but she doesn't answer so I walk down the stairs, still drying my hair.

The door to Brian's room is cracked. I say Tracy's name again, secretly hoping she'll come out so I don't have to go in there, but she doesn't. I push open the door and walk onto his ugly beige carpet.

Tracy doesn't even turn around when I walk in. She just stands there, staring at his bed with her eyes slitted and her nostrils flared and this look on her face that's really really far away. Brian's bed is unmade, you can see his imprint in it, and the carpet suddenly feels itchy and gross under my bare feet. I keep walking toward Tracy. When I get up close I can see her cheeks are wet and it's not from the shower because the rest of her is dry. She's breathing hard like some kind of little animal and I say her name again, this time super soft like a whisper almost, and she snaps her head up and around to look at me and her whole face rearranges. She inhales hard, then closes her eyes and shakes her head. When she opens her eyes again she grabs my arm. "Come on" she says. "Let's go raid the fridge."

We leave with both our backpacks full of chips and cereal and peanut butter, bread and carrots, plus a jug of water and two sleeping bags. Tracy went through the drawers too and when she found this little knife small enough to fit in a pocket she told me to take it; I wrapped it in a paper towel and slipped it into my jeans. I keep feeling it. I took some twenties too from Linda's room, memorizing how the bras were stacked and putting them back exactly perfect. I gave the money to Tracy right away; I thought she'd want to carry it. I cleaned everything up better than I've ever cleaned before, threw our towels in the hamper and rearranged the fridge so they wouldn't see the empty parts. I didn't even go into my room.

I lock the door behind us; Tracy watches while I put the key back down beneath the plastic rock. As soon as it's out of my hands I realize the thing I was scared of didn't happen: I went back in the house without it changing me back to how I was. I even went in Brian's room and the only thing I thought about in there was Tracy. All of a sudden I feel really light even though my backpack's ten pounds heavier.

After that I decide I don't really want to go back. Or actually it's not a decision exactly, it's more of a realization. The whole last week I was procrastinating on going home like it was a math worksheet and every once in a while I'd hear Linda's annoying voice in my head yelling at me for putting things off and my heart would get all poundy knowing I'd have to do it eventually and the longer I waited the worse it would get. But now all of a sudden it's like my math teacher canceled the assignment and I just don't have to do it. Coming down the hill and back toward Hollywood I'm someone different from Elly who goes to school and eats in the cafeteria and sits in class and comes home at night and tells Dad and Linda how my day was. I'm so much bigger now and beautiful and I can go back to the house and just take what I want when they're gone and I even have a different name. I'm never going back.

Tracy's got a ring through her left nostril which I think looks really pretty, even though the metal's sort of greenish. I told her I wanted one too and she said that was lame but how about my lip. So we went back to Rite Aid to steal some safety pins, peroxide and a ring and now we're on the sidewalk across from Del Taco. I can taste the peroxide bubbling on my gums and I wonder if it's poisonous. It tastes like eggs and rust.

She's making me hold my lower lip out while she gets the pin ready; it makes it hard to talk so when I ask her about the guys sitting in the parking lot in front of 7-Eleven right across the street it comes out sounding like some retarded other language. She laughs and says "Hang on" and stabs the safety pin through the middle of my lip, fast. My head fills all the way up with the pain of it and my whole mouth tastes like liquid iron. I blink my eyes really hard so it won't look like I'm crying while she screws the pin around trying to close it. Finally she does and it squinches my lip but only a little because we got the big kind. The bottom of it knocks against my chin. "Leave that in for a day or two and then we'll put the ring in," she says, and wipes her hands off on her jeans. "Now what were you trying to say?"

"I was just wondering if you knew those guys" I say, swallowing blood, and point over to the 7-Eleven lot. There's two of them with a pit bull there, both dressed like Tracy, patches and black pants and splotchy dirty brown T-shirts, which is why I think she might know them. The dog's got two collars, one with rhinestones, one with spikes, and you can see its ribs.

She looks over at them for a second and goes "Nah." Sometimes Tracy lies about stuff like that but I can tell it's true she doesn't know them, and it's obvious she doesn't really want to. Which I think is kind of weird, in the same way as the smoking kids behind the auditorium: if you're a person that looks different from everyone and you see someone who looks like you, to me that means you'd want to be friends or at least talk. But not Tracy.

I'm curious about the guys, though, so I watch them. They're both around Tracy's age, and the really tall and skinny one with the stocking cap has this perfect face like someone in the movies, green-eyed and almost pretty like a girl's. The dog is sitting down and so's the other guy; he's short and strong and he looks sort of jocky even though he's got freckles and tattoos and dirty patches on his hoodie. The dog belongs to him, I can tell.

I never saw anyone else who looked like Tracy and I can't stop watching them.

I'm still staring across the street when Tracy reaches over and flicks the safety pin in my lip, which hurts like shit. "Come on," she says. "Come buy me a donut," and even though there's food left in her backpack from my house I follow her.

That night and the next day and the next I keep trying to get Tracy to go to Del Taco instead of Benito's hoping we'll see those guys again across the street, but they don't show up and after a couple days I forget. Something in me is different, though, just knowing they exist. To me it means there's a whole bunch of people like her, which means the world is bigger than I knew. It means there's something out there that's not school or home or Brian but not Tracy either. It's like Tracy, but it's not exactly her. For some reason, that makes me feel a little more equal, like I could ask her questions without being scared that she'll get mad. I don't know why.

Also I keep thinking about Brian's room, how I found Tracy in there staring at his bed and crying, the way she held my hand beneath the 101 after I told her and looked at me like I was someone she'd known forever but hadn't seen since we were little kids. The rest of the time she never holds my hand or even touches me but it felt really good that time she did and I keep wanting it again.

One morning after rush hour when Tang's Donut is empty and we've had two apple fritters plus leftover Boston cremes from yesterday, I bring it up. I keep picking at my nails and my jeans which are getting pretty brown. There's a hole starting in one knee; I make it bigger thread by thread. What I really want to ask is: was she crying inside Brian's room and why, but I think that she might kill me if I do. So I just say "How come you were so nice to me before?" which doesn't make any sense, and of course she asks me what the fuck I'm talking about and I have to explain I mean on the way to my house when I told her about Brian. Personally I think it's kind of obvious after that, but she looks at me and goes "What do you mean? I wasn't nice to you."

I rip the rest of the apple fritter up into little tiny pieces; it looks like donut turds. Then I try to explain: I mean when I told her about Brian and looking at the ceiling, how it started in fourth grade and at first it was nice having him in bed with me and then it started getting scary and by the end of that year I'd start throwing up the closer it got to bedtime. I mean when I explained how I could never tell Linda because all she cares about is her stupid job and Brian, and I can't tell my dad either, even though I kind of wish I could, because if he ever believed me it would mean he'd have to kick Brian out, which might make Linda leave, and I'd mess everything up and everyone would hate me. I feel like a major asshole going through it all again, especially when the donut pieces get too small to rip up anymore. I start back in on the hole in my jeans but she's still not talking so finally I look up at her and she's crying again, not like normal where you can hear it and the person moves their face, but in this weird way where her eyes are like a statue and she's hardly even breathing.

It's like two things are fighting in her face: one, she keeps almost opening it up like she really wants to say something or touch me; but the other, she is really, really mad. And the first thing I think is: she knows it's kind of my fault that it happened. She feels bad for me, which is the first thing in her face and why she was so nice before; but I'm so stupid for it happening, and even stupider to want to tell my dad, and that's the other thing. It doesn't explain the crying but it's all I can think of so I think it must be true. "I'm sorry," I go, and really mean it. She doesn't talk for a long time. "Don't be sorry," she says, and then stands up and grabs me and we go out into the street.

That night we sleep behind Whole Foods again. Halfway through the night I wake up and Tracy is curled up around me, pressed into me through our sleeping bags. She's on her side, her bony arm across my chest, holding tight, breathing loud. I wiggle sideways toward her so she won't have to work so hard to hold on.

That morning she doesn't look at me the whole way to Tang's Donut. She doesn't say much either and at first I think she might be embarrassed. I try to keep my hands and knees away from her so there'll be a cushion of space between us in case I was touching her too much last night. When she comes back from the counter with the bag she takes three donuts for herself and only gives me the dried-out cinnamon one with the powder half worn off. Usually we split them and I get jelly or a fritter or at least glazed. She keeps picking at some scab or something on her head and looking everywhere except at me.

I try asking her different questions. What time is it, and what does she want to do today, and how much cash do we have left. She just looks around and picks at things and gives me just enough answers to make me stop asking. She seems mad and I think maybe she doesn't like me anymore, now that she thinks the whole Brian thing is my fault. I want to ask her if it's true but I'm too afraid to hear the answer. I tell myself there are a lot of things that could be wrong besides that though: I go through them in my head picking them up and looking at them like different-colored rocks, trying to find one I can put in my pocket and keep, but that one reason I'm scared of is underneath all of them rotting into the dirt and every time I pick another one up I can see it.

I feel like a big asshole even though nothing's even happened; it sort of reminds me of school, except worse. I pick at my shoelace and get really involved in it. Tracy picks at her scalp. After a minute I think we must look pretty weird, both sitting on the curb in front of Tang's picking at things and not talking, but then I realize nobody's looking at us.

The rest of the day is a mixture of picking at shoelaces and sitting on curbs, and in between Tracy is dragging me like it's really important to all these places where she thinks someone might be. She doesn't say who. I hope it might be those guys from the 7-Eleven with the pit bull but I think she'd tell me if it was. We go to Jack in the Box up on Sunset and then back to Winchell's and Del Taco; she's looking for something but she won't explain what. At Benito's she walks right up to this transvestite hooker from before. I can't stop looking at her face. She's wearing leopard print and purple high heels. Also she's about seven feet tall. Her name's Bianca. She tilts her face down and asks, in a Spanish accent, what a little sweetie like me is doing out here and then she sort of glares at Tracy. Tracy shoves in front of me and starts talking to Bianca half in Spanish so I can't understand, and then she grabs my sleeve and marches me away, and then we go and stand outside Goodwill for like half an hour. No one comes.

Every time she says we're going to find some person

and it's like she really needs to see them but there isn't ever anybody there. There's no talking, just a big swollen-up embarrassed silence in the air between us. My stomach is nervous and sick at the same time, like butterflies and throw-up, and I wish I could get in bed and stay home from school, but there's nothing to stay home from and no home to stay in either.

After a while she doesn't even seem mad anymore, just like some other person in some place that isn't here. I'm still here though, out on the asphalt, and without her I don't know where here is or where to put my feet. For the first time since she led me out of the parking lot at school I feel really scared. Tracy's always had a reason or a kind of knowing, and even when I can't tell what it is it wraps around me like her arms last night and leads me to the next right thing. But today I can't find it. All morning I tried talking and it just made her weirder so now I've been trying to find her just by feeling it, like if I breathe the right way our breaths will touch and I can pull her close again. But my stomach hurts too bad for me to breathe in deep enough to make it work, so I just wait at each place she takes me and then follow her to the next one even though I can tell we're not really going anywhere.

Finally the sky gets halfway dark and we head back to Whole Foods. My stomach starts to calm down: that's our place, we go there every night; there's not ever anyone there but us. I hate today. The whole day just blended into itself, different in a way I can't say the name of, and I want something back that I don't even know what it is. Whole Foods makes me feel better though. When we're sleeping I won't have to think of anything to say and then tomorrow morning the cars will come and the light before the sun comes up and it'll be like today just didn't happen.

For dinner we get muffins from the trash bags: tonight it's cranberry almond. It's weird how much food they just throw away and I'm glad there's somebody hungry like us to eat it, otherwise it'd just turn into trash. Linda always shops here and I wonder if she knows we're back by the Dumpsters eating all the stuff she doesn't want to buy. I imagine her car full of grocery bags curving around the tiny hilly streets to get back home and then I think about our driveway, the birds of paradise and bougainvillea clustered up around the door. I think about all that stuff while we're eating. When we lie down in our sleeping bags, I turn my back to Tracy. I don't want her to know I'm at my house in my head and not here with her. I can feel her watching me, though, and after a while she pokes me. I roll over and she's propped up on one elbow staring at my face. Her eyes are full like she wants to say something but she doesn't. I almost ask her what, but I'm afraid if I talk it'll break something. After a long time she picks up her hand and wipes my hair away from my eyes and off my forehead, soft, in this way that's almost like a mom except awkward, like her hands aren't supposed to move that way. It's weird but I like it and

I stop thinking about our driveway. She keeps on doing it until I fall asleep.

The next morning when the cars start and the sun comes up the space next to me is empty and her stuff is gone. There's nothing there to look at except asphalt and a Dumpster that's all emptied out. It smells like muffins baking and my stomach growls.

rusty

"*hold up!*" *this voice yells from behind me and I* almost jump out of my skin. I don't know if it's a cop or what till I turn around and see the stringy blond-haired girl, halfway across the parking lot, careening up to the car like some crazy bird with half a wing. I recognize her face: I've seen her around the corner on Pacific, a little past the liquor store next to the beach; she's the only other one out here in Venice near my age. But now out of nowhere she's running in five directions at once, toward me and the guy in the car, who hasn't even told me his name yet. He's old, and at first he looks nervous, but then she catches up and throws her arm around my shoulder, squeezing her face next to mine so it's me and her in his open window and I can feel her heavy breath. "You taking good care of my baby brother?" she asks the guy and when he nods, his eyes all wide, she grins and says "I'm Tracy. You wanna take care of me too?" I start to say something, but the guy leans over to open the passenger door so we both just get in.

She shoves me over so I'm on the brown pleather hump pressed into him. I fumble for a seat belt, but the one in the middle is half stuck down in the seat and won't come out. While I'm tugging, she leans into me quick and soft and whispers "My name's Tracy; we're from Fresno and I'm two years older." Then she leans back, rests her feet up on the glove compartment, and points her face into the breeze.

I've only been doing this a couple weeks. When I got off the Greyhound from Bakersfield a month ago I had two hundred bucks and Jim's number crumpled up in my pocket. I'd had it memorized for practically a year but he insisted on writing it down, like he wanted to make sure nothing got in the way of him finding me to start our new life in L.A. He gave me everything I might need, toothpaste and money and a map, and he told me to stay in a hostel and call him every night till he came. He wished he could drive us to the city in his convertible Volkswagen and get us our own place first thing, but he said they might come find us if he quit with no notice on the same day that I ran away.

Jim is the choir teacher at Bakersfield High and we've been in love since spring of ninth grade. It was perfect and secret for eight months, till my mom came home early from work and saw his Cabriolet pull out of our driveway. She stopped talking to me then and started going through my shit, and even though I hid everything he ever wrote me, Jim was nervous. After he heard her click onto the line one night when we were talking, he said we'd have to go some-place else if we wanted to stay together.

It wasn't much of a choice: Jim and I are in love. He's the only person who knows who I am in the places that you can't put into words, those places that are alive and raw and secret, and bigger than your regular life. We all have those places, I think, but we almost never see or touch them in each other because everyone is always scared. But Jim's not scared: he's big enough to hold every single part of me, and brave enough to show me himself. We had sex for the first time at the end of ninth grade in the choir room and after-ward he held me on the brown carpet and told me he was all I'd ever need and I breathed in the rough smell of his neck and knew that it was true.

So the fact that he hasn't answered his phone since the day after I got here is weird, and I'm worried that something happened to him. Every night I call Jim on the pay phone and let it ring twenty times till the operator comes on and says "Your party is not answering. Please try your call again later." Every time I pray while it's ringing that Jim will pick up, but I guess I haven't learned how to pray well enough yet, because it keeps just being the operator.

It's been a month now since I left and we were only plan-ning for a week, so the money Jim gave me ran out a while ago. I'm too young to get a job, so I was getting really hungry till one night in Hollywood by the hostel a guy asked me if I needed cash and I said yes. It was scary getting in his car, but he parked nearby beneath some trees and all he wanted was to touch me. I closed my eyes and thought about the apartment Jim was going to get us when he got here and the bed we'd have. At the end I told Jim I was sorry in my head, but I knew he'd understand I was just waiting for him.

The second guy brought me over to his place in Santa Monica. I watched the ocean from his window and afterward I walked out his door and toward the sea and down the beach till I got to Venice. The sun setting turned the sky orange and the ocean black. The air was open in my lungs and there were seagulls and I thought maybe I could make some money over here instead of Hollywood, where the air was thick and close and way too hot. I walked the boardwalk while the hippies packed up their bad paintings into RVs and the T-shirt stores closed, then I crisscrossed the alleys in the dark till I saw people standing around who looked kind of like me.

So here's where I've been the last couple weeks: on Pacific and Navy by the liquor store, or else in the parks by the boardwalk. It's not too bad sleeping outside, not like Hollywood where it's hard and dirty and every place you go is full of trash. Here at least there's grass and sand: every night I feel the ground against my cheek and imagine it's the brown rug in the choir room.

I've never gone so long without talking to anyone, though. To the guys I never say more than my name and what do they want and that I'm eighteen, which is a lie, and none of that really counts as conversation. I miss Jim so much it feels like a clamp twisting inside my chest. Closing my eyes to think of him when I'm working helped at first, but now it's starting to make it worse. So even though I don't really know what Tracy's doing here in the car, taking up so much of the seat that I'm straddling the hump and paranoid my bony knees will knock the gearshift, I'm kind of glad she's sitting next to me.

I keep looking at my lap. I'm embarrassed to talk to the guy with Tracy here, which is weird because I can tell she does the same things I do. The silence gets dense and the guy drives and finally Tracy leans forward and goes "So don't you want to know where we're from?" He looks relieved that somebody's talking to him and he says "Yeah," so Tracy goes into this whole story about Fresno and how we slept in the same bed growing up and came to L.A. together for adventures. I guess I can see the resemblance— we're both pale and skinny enough that our ribs poke out— but I still feel like the guy is going to know I'm not her brother. My hair is brown, not blond like hers, and besides I think he'll just be able to smell it. I want her to shut up, but she just keeps talking about our bed.

She elbows me at the end of her story like I'm supposed to say something. I don't know what to say, so I just go "Yup" and look up at the guy all dumb. Tracy laughs and says "He's really shy" and makes this face like they're on the same team and they're planning something about me. For a minute I get scared, and then Tracy leans back and pulls me toward her and I can tell it's really me and her on the team.

We're at the guy's house a little less than an hour. His place is gross, with stacked-up newspapers on the scratchy orange couch and just mustard in the refrigerator. And he's older than my dad, like fifty or something, so it makes me this weird creepy kind of sad. Not for very long though, because Tracy grabs my baggy T-shirt and yanks me into the back hallway by the bathroom. She pulls out four cans of Campbell's soup she's stuck in her backpack, plus a package of ramen. She's got two lighters too, and says one of them's for me. She's good: I never saw her open any drawers.

After a minute the guy hollers out to us from the living room. My heart starts pounding because of the Campbell's and ramen, but Tracy zips her bag up slow; when she's ready she pulls me out into the living room and toward the couch.

Before the guy can talk I tell him I won't use anything but my hands. Tracy shoots me a look for a second like I really fucked up, but then a smirk flickers over her face like a mask and she goes "I told you he's shy. It's cute, right?" The guy sort of half nods and doesn't look mad so then she smiles at me.

I'm nervous around a girl, especially since the lights are on and Tracy's just sitting there like she's not planning to do anything except sit there and watch, but I go for his belt anyway, because that's what we're there for. Then she starts talking. She goes "He's always been that way, ever since he was little," and the guy closes his eyes like it's all part of the same thing, her story and my hands, like he's expecting her to start in on something sexy. But it starts turning into this weird long made-up thing about when we were kids, like the stuff your mom told you at bedtime when she was out of books to read and couldn't think of what to say. When I finally look up at Tracy, she's got this huge grin on her face and I snort out this giant sudden almost laugh. I swallow it fast but she makes the story weirder and weirder trying to get me to crack up and pretty soon I've got tears streaming down my cheeks from holding it in and I want to pee. I have to look at the wall; if I look at Tracy's face again we'll both lose our shit. Already the guy's eyelids are twitching like this wasn't what he expected and maybe he should stop and make sure everything's okay. But he lets me keep going. At the end I don't wait to hear the rest of Tracy's story: I just get up super fast and run to the bathroom and she grabs her bag and follows me and we run the water full on while we both laugh so hard it hurts our stomachs and doesn't make any sound. After a second we calm down and I wash my hands with crappy liquid soap. Then she gives me this look in the streaky gray mirror and we both crack up again.

Afterward Tracy takes the money, drops me off at the liquor store and goes to get some Baja Fresh. She says she'll bring me back fish tacos, but without anyone to talk to I close my eyes and start thinking about Jim again and wind up falling asleep sitting up against the side of the building and wake up with drool all down my chin. When I open my eyes it's late and I'm confused like when you lie down for a nap during the day and by the time you wake up it's pitch black outside and the time in the middle just erased itself. Tracy never showed up with those tacos. I'm starving. I think maybe I should be pissed at her. I walk over to the beach so I can at least sleep somewhere soft.

The next guy who picks me up wants to take me to West Hollywood. He's in a Lexus, jocky like he's probably got a girlfriend that he's mean to, but I go with him. Before I get in I do one more check to see if Tracy's anywhere, even though I can see she's not. Just in case she'd want to come.

He drives all the way east on Santa Monica with the windows down and the strip malls flicker by, their signs lit up even though they're closed, the too-bright plastic lights against the black. Even the strip malls here are full of things hiding just behind where you can see, like if you reached past the outsides of them you could touch a thousand things you never knew. The air's a mix of car exhaust and ocean; wind whips my hair against my cheeks. It hurts just enough to make me feel awake and I miss Jim. I wonder if he misses me the same, and then it scares me that I'm even wondering, so I tell myself *Of course he does*, and push away the question. The lights blink way into the distance, all the way out to Bakersfield and past it; if you look far enough you can't tell the difference between lightbulbs and stars.

It's quiet for so long I'm surprised when the guy talks to me, but he does, tells me to get out of the car and come in, asks me if I want a beer and tells me what he wants, and then doesn't talk again for a long time. Afterward he says to leave because he's got people coming over, and doesn't let me finish the beer.

Outside his street is full of little squat houses, orange and yellow and green; they all look like sherbet and have trimmed lawns with agave plants and bougainvillea growing right up to the row of shiny cars. Every ten feet there's another sign that says NO PARKING THIS BLOCK WITHOUT PERMIT; it makes me wonder who gets all those permits and what the rest of everyone's supposed to do. It doesn't bug me, though; all I've got is my feet and I'm sure when Jim gets here he'll be able to park his Cabriolet wherever he wants. I walk through no-parking streets to Melrose where there's pay phones and I let Jim's number ring till it gets dark.

Starting that night I stay in Hollywood. Venice is better, but I can't find anyone to drive me back and it's far and I don't know the bus routes. I'm tired, too, from strangers and car fumes and waiting. Before Jim I always wished I didn't have to go to school, but now I'm realizing how hard it is to find something to do all day long if you don't have a place to go. Every time I find something like go to Starbucks it only lasts an hour or two and then I'm back at zero with a Frappuccino sitting in my stomach, looking for another thing, and no one ever talks to me. It kind of makes me understand jobs.

There's no beach to sleep on in Hollywood, so I check into the hostel on Vine, lay down on the stiff white sheets and think of Jim. When it's quiet and I close my eyes I can see invisible cords that cross the highways and the hills, stretching out between me and him and tying us together. They tug at the middle of my chest, make it ache, but I'm still glad they're there. Sometimes I roll over and stare at the space beside me on the bed, picturing he's filling it, and some nights on the pay phone I imagine his voice in the space between the rings.

Besides that I'm alone. I'm trying not to pick anybody up: in Hollywood the air is like an oven and it feels like I could crawl into the back of some guy's car and never get let out. I guess it's really like that everywhere no matter how it feels, but I try not to think about that. Between not working and the hostel I'm almost out of money. One dollar and seventy-three cents left.

There's a kind of hungry that's way past stomach growling that I've only ever felt since I came to L.A. The empty inside you expands like it's an actual thing instead of just a space; then it pushes against you from the inside, steady, till it starts to hurt. The bubbles turn to rocks, holding your insides apart, and after a while you can't tell the difference between too full and too empty. You don't feel what's going on inside you anymore, just that something's wrong. And even if you eat, it doesn't go away for hours.

I've been trying to save my buck seventy-three for an emergency, but I'm starting to really need food and my throat's so dry it's sticking to itself. I can't afford the taco stands so I walk west on Santa Monica, knowing eventually I'll hit a 7-Eleven, where microwave burritos are eighty-nine cents and I can get a soda too. Once my stomach is calm I'll be able to think; then maybe I can stick out my thumb like in the movies and some old guy will take pity on my plight and drive me back to Venice.

By the time I push through the door, past the magazine racks full of *Variety* and *Hollywood Reporter*, I'm dizzy enough that it's hard to find my way around the store. I know burritos are always back by the Big Gulps, but my eyes are blurry and sped-up enough that I go the wrong way and brush into a tower of chips. The guy at the counter's eyes flick up from *People* magazine as soon as I knock into the chip bags, and they stay on me. When I finally find my way through the plastic junk food maze, he hollers back at me to pay before I microwave and I have to say "What?" twice before I understand because he's from Pakistan or someplace. I feel stupid for not deciphering his accent, like I might offend him; my face gets hot and I know it's turning pink. I bring the burrito up to the counter and a big Mountain Dew for caffeine. I can't look at him but I can tell his eyes are still stuck to my face and hands. They dart back and forth as I count out my change on the scuffed white Formica.

He rings me up and it comes out to a dollar ninety-three. Even before I'm done counting I know I don't have it, but I keep sliding nickels and dimes across from one hand to the other so I can act like it's a surprise. Finally I get to the end and go "Oh shit!" and look up and blink like *Oops, I forgot the rest of my money in the car* or something. He just looks at me and says "One dollar ninety-three cents."

"I'm short. Twenty cents. Can I owe you?" I say and make my eyes as wide as I can without twitching.

"One dollar ninety-three cents," he says.

"Come on," I go. It's not like it's going to kill him. There are spots in front of everything and I'm starting to feel like I need to eat like *right now*.

"Sorry." He shrugs.

"Come on!" I say. "It's twenty cents!" He looks at me like a concrete wall and raises his eyebrows. I wait for him to answer.

"Sorry," he goes again, in the exact same identical monotone as before.

I've never gotten mad at a stranger or especially a

grown-up, but the empty in my stomach has spread to my head. "It's twenty fucking cents!" I go. "I'm hungry! Just let me have it!" and I'm kind of yelling.

"Please quiet down, sir," he tells me and his voice is like a rock.

"Don't call me fucking sir!" I yell louder, and I can feel hot tears rolling down the dry of my cheeks and all of a sudden my nose is full of snot. The guy and the counter and the cigarettes and the hot-dog machine on the counter all go blurry and I can't even read the red numbers on the register anymore; I'm just crying and swearing and I don't even know why or what I'm saying.

Then the guy is around on my side of the counter and he's got his big hand in the middle of my back, covering my spine, and his spread-out fingers reach almost across both my shoulder blades. My bones feel like a bird beneath his hand and I feel like if I fell back it'd catch me except he's pushing me toward the door hard enough to make me trip over my feet and if I don't watch out I'll fly right into the glass. "Don't come back," he says and now his voice is mean and a new wave of tears and snot comes up from my chest. I shove into the door with my shoulder and stumble away from the hot push of his hand.

On the pavement the first thing I realize is I left my fucking change on the counter, all seventy-three cents, and my ribs jerk in and out again and I crumple down onto the pebbly gravel of the parking lot.

"Hey," someone says above me, and I can hardly even lift my head to look—I can't take one more thing. If it's a cop or some guy hitting on me I think I'll break into a million pieces and turn to dust. I nod just enough to let him know I heard him, though, so nobody can call me rude. "That guy never cuts anyone a break. I saw through the window. You hungry?"

His voice is nice enough to make the crying wear off for a second; I rub my eyes and look up. It's just this kid. He's my age I think and about my height, five eight or so, but bigger. He's got the opposite body of me: instead of straight-up-and-down skinny, he's broad through the shoulders and solid, almost stocky, with dark brown hair cut really short and freckles—and he's dressed like a whole other world. His T-shirt and shorts are faded black like they've been in the sun for a year and he's got patches sewn on everywhere and a knife strapped to his belt loop in a leather case that looks like he made it himself. Down by his boots there's a big army bag, and tied to the bag is a piece of long dirty rope, and at the end of the rope is a brown pit bull, panting. He smiles at me. "I'll be right back. You watch the dog?"

I nod and he goes into the 7-Eleven. The counter guy glares but doesn't say anything, and I watch through the window as the kid microwaves two burritos and buys them and a Mountain Dew. When he gets his change back he looks at it and says something I can't hear. Then the

58

counter guy opens the register again and gives him three more quarters.

He comes back out, sits down next to the dog, and says "Thanks." I must look scared because he goes "Germ's friendly. He won't hurt you." I've never heard of a dog named Germ, but okay. He hands me the bag with the burritos. "I thought you could maybe use two."

All the water that was in my eyes before is in my mouth now. I'm starving. I tell him thanks and take the bag, trying not to snatch it out of his hands and rip it open. He watches me and smiles. "My name's Squid," he says.

My mouth is so full I can barely chew, let alone talk. I try to say my name, but instead I make some weird kind of grunty noise and then my face turns red. I'm such a loser. "It's cool," he goes, and kind of laughs. "You can tell me after."

After I choke down both burritos and chug half the Mountain Dew I feel like maybe I can breathe again. I have no idea why this guy is being nice to me. "Thanks" is the only thing I can think of to say, but it seems like not enough. He just smiles at me again. He keeps smiling. I don't know if I'm funny or what. "I'm Rusty," I remember to tell him.

"Cool," he goes. "Where you from?" I tell him Bakersfield. I start to explain more, but then remember that I can't: Jim always said no one should find out, no matter if they're someone we know or not. I sort of trail off in the middle but Squid doesn't seem to notice; he just nods and says "I hear Bakersfield sucks." He doesn't tell me where he's from. Germ pants some more and I pet him.

"Oh," Squid goes and reaches into his pocket. "I almost forgot." He hands me three quarters. "This is yours."

"Thanks," I go, and take the change; then I realize I haven't spent any money but I still just ate. "Do you want—" I start to say, but he interrupts me.

"Nah. It's cool." I keep watching him to see if he's expecting something else from me, but he just pets the dog.

We hang out in the parking lot till the sky starts turning pink. Once in a while the 7-Eleven guy comes over and glares at us through the window; when he does, Squid reaches out his arm without even looking and hits the glass hard with the back of his hand. It always makes the guy go away.

That nervous feeling of not having something to do doesn't happen when there's another person there. Whenever the silence gets too long you can ask the other person questions and they'll fill it up for you. After a while Squid says where he's from, which is Arizona, and that he's been in L.A. since last year. He's sixteen. It sort of scares me that someone could live like this for a whole year without anything changing, especially when he asks me how long I've been here and I hear myself tell him a month and a half. It was only supposed to be a week.

Before I can think about that too much I ask him how

he got here and he says "Trains." I think he means Amtrak, but then he describes it: he snuck into the backs of freight trains and rode them for free, hidden out with his ex-girlfriend Annabelle. When they ran away they headed toward L.A. instead of Austin because the train to Texas runs near Mexico and INS will take you to jail. It doesn't matter if you're American or not; if you don't pay they'll come on the train and get you. So they went the other way. She came all the way to California with him, he says, and then a couple weeks went by and she met a guy who took her up to Berkeley. He sort of stops for a second when he tells me that part and I want to ask him about it, but I don't know what to say.

I can't believe the train thing, though. I never heard of anyone doing that except in movies, and never a kid. I didn't even know there were such things as freight trains anymore. All of a sudden his face turns into something out of a storybook and I have about a hundred million questions I want to ask, but he says "C'mon. Let's go meet my friends" and pulls me up by the elbow. Germ perks up his ears like we're on an adventure.

We go down Hollywood a few blocks to this taco stand Benito's. On the way I'm nervous and I wish that Jim was here; he always knows how to act and what to do. When we get close, Squid waves at two kids sitting on the dirty orange stools; I fall in step behind him as we walk up to them. The guy's named Critter and he's really tall and skinny with a stocking cap on top and has a face like nothing I've ever seen before except for on a billboard or a magazine. It's almost like a girl's, so beautiful, with all the bones lined up, pronounced and delicate, his long dark eyelashes ringing bright green eyes. I try not to stare. He nods at me and I sort of lift my chin at him but then I look at my feet.

The girl says "Hey" to me, sort of too loud like she's trying to prove she's there. She's short, so I don't have to raise my head too much to meet her eyes; when I do she looks me up and down in this way that's supposed to seem brave but is obviously jumpy underneath. She can't be older than thirteen. She's got short magenta hair that looks like she cut it herself and a ring through her lip, and she's chunky. Her clothes are cleaner than the rest of them, and her backpack is the kind you use for school, not camping. "I'm Eeyore," she goes, and then she leans back into Critter and looks up at him.

"Eeyore just started hanging out with us," Squid goes. "Right?" he asks her, and she sort of seems embarrassed that it hasn't been very long. I don't know why she would be; I just met them today.

"Couple weeks," she goes.

Squid laughs. "More like a couple days." Eeyore looks at the sidewalk, mad. "We found her back behind Whole Foods when we were Dumpstering. She like memorized their whole schedule. This kid knows how to get the good shit." All of a sudden a big grin takes over Eeyore's face; she sticks out her chest a little and beams up at Critter. Squid shoots me a look like he did it on purpose.

After a couple days, Germ starts to wag his tail when I talk to him. It's nice being recognized; it hasn't happened in a while. Not since Bakersfield. It's exhausting to always only see brand-new faces and corners and sidewalks, to never get to settle on one, rest your eyes and feel like home. It wears you out. When I picture Jim in my head there's this mad feeling that's starting to mix in with the worry, but I still keep imagining him anyway, just because he's the only thing I can really remember, the only thing that lets me know where I am.

But now Germ knows me, and Squid starts feeling familiar to me too: I know what he smells like and the sound of his voice. I have a little place to rest, even if it's only small. Critter and Eeyore come and go some, but Squid is always there. He never leaves me alone. I memorize him fast; hanging out with him just feels sort of normal and he smiles at me so much I never worry about saying the wrong thing. One time I went off to find a pay phone, but I told him I was going to the bathroom. But everything else I can say.

I've done a good job with stretching my last dollar out: Eeyore's always bringing us free food from trash cans I don't know where, and Squid taught me to sleep in the alleys. I'd never spend the night out there alone—I'd feel so naked and peeled open I'd never be able to sleep—but with the rest of them around it's okay. Kind of like camping, except without a tent or a fire or trees. Sometimes we go behind Whole Foods where you can smell the warm sugar of the bakery through the vents, or else in alleys by Benito's. It's never quiet enough to close my eyes and imagine Jim like in the hostel, but the rest of them fill the space laughing so usually I don't feel it much. Eeyore and Critter huddle up in the middle of everyone: she curls into him like a little sister and he keeps her warm. Squid and I say good night to each other over the lump the two of them make and I soak in the heat across them.

After the first few days Eeyore quits talking so loud all the time, and as long as I don't stand too close to Critter she's sweet to me. When she's not trying hard to stand up the tallest, you can see what she actually looks like: really young and like a baby bird, with all these soft spots that aren't covered up by anything. I know that feeling. I have them too. I want to tell her she doesn't have to put all that stupid hard stuff over them, that those spots are beautiful and the way to be safe is to find somebody who will touch them, not to cover them up. But she'd probably take it wrong.

It's been a week of me hanging out with them when Critter goes to meet some guy one night and comes back with a backpack full of junk, which I've never seen before.

I'm actually not even sure what kind of drug junk is, although I know it's something serious. I want to ask him if I can look at it but I know he'll think I'm stupid, so I don't. In the morning Critter says he's gonna go unload the junk at Hollywood and Highland. Squid nods like it's normal, but Eeyore's eyes ping-pong up at Critter like she thinks he'll never come back. Right away he asks her if she wants to come. She jumps up so fast she almost falls back down, and he holds out his hand in case she needs to balance. She doesn't take it, even though you can tell she wants to.

They don't come back that afternoon or night, or the next morning either. Squid doesn't seem worried, but I am: I'm thinking about food. I don't know any place to Dumpster besides Whole Foods and usually we don't go that far west; I guess I got used to Eeyore doing it for us. And Squid always seems to have money, but I can't ask him to pay for me. The one thing I could give him in return he wouldn't want, and when you ask for stuff and don't give back, people start wanting you to go away. Squid buys me a chicken and bean burrito without me asking the first morning they're not back; it lasts me till it's almost dark, but then I start getting that solid empty feeling in my stomach again.

That night Squid drinks a 40 and passes out in the alley. I lie there looking up at the moon and the stars and the helicopters, my hunger pangs too sharp for me to fall asleep, and realize I have to make some money.

Jim promised he'd show up before my cash ran out, and

when I think about it I get really pissed that he hasn't. A jolt runs through me like my blood is speeding up; it almost makes my stomach sick. But then I tell myself there has to be a reason, something that happened that's keeping him away from his phone, and the pissed-off turns to worry, which is familiar and a whole lot better. I try to hang on to that feeling, keep it from switching back and scaring me again. My blood calms down and I remember that the thing I have to do is keep myself okay until he finds me. That's what Jim said.

It wouldn't be hard to work from here: it's where I started anyway. Probably if I found a corner and stood out there a couple days I could make enough to live on for a week and even buy Squid a couple burritos. The problem is I have friends now. Squid is with me every day; he'd come looking if I left. He knows every corner and cross street in Hollywood, and if I stayed around here, he'd come find me.

When I imagine that, I feel like I've got dirt coating all my skin that won't wash off and I look over at Squid, scared I'll wake him just by picturing it. I know he wouldn't hate me for it but he'd probably be grossed out and that's worse. And it's weird but I also feel this thing like it'd kind of be cheating on him, which is bizarre because I have a boyfriend, and even though he's all the way back in Bakersfield, never picking up his phone, I haven't ever felt like I was cheating on *him*.

I figure if Squid can sneak onto trains all across the

country, I can ride a bus. And so in the morning when Squid goes for coffee I say I'm still sleepy, and while he's gone I spange a dollar and get on the first bus going west. I ride it all the way to Venice. It takes two hours, but I finally get off at Rose and Pacific, three blocks from the liquor store parking lot, and when I walk up who of course is sitting there drinking out of a brown paper bag in broad daylight but Tracy.

"Hey." I go up to her and kick her boot. "I think you owe me some fish tacos." She looks up at me with this blank mean sleepy look that I've never seen before; it sort of scares me. But after about three seconds she sees who I am, and a big grin washes over her face and her eyes wake up again.

"What's up!" She jumps to her feet and throws her arms around my neck. Her beer bottle hits the base of my skull but not too hard and I sort of laugh, surprised at getting hit but also that she's so happy to see me. She takes a little step back and appraises me, like I've seen guys do sometimes when I'm working, except she puts a twinkle behind it. "You want fish tacos, you have to earn 'em, sweetie," she says to me. "Let's get to work."

That whole day we're like a factory: four tricks, one after the other. I'd never be able to do that many by myself, but with her I can. The first three guys stop for me and she tags along; they're weirded out that Tracy's there but she acts like it's so normal I guess they feel like they can't say anything. She

67

doesn't tell crazy stories like before, which to tell you the truth I'm a little disappointed, but she's fun the whole time. Even though it's embarrassing doing stuff in front of a girl, it's way easier with her there. I don't feel the kind of pushed-down scared alone I usually do, trying to make my face tough so the guys won't be mean. With her around, my eyes relax and no one can hurt me. Tracy's knees-and-elbows skinny, but having her in the backseat is like sleeping curled up beside Germ: it's always good to have someone next to you who bites. Also, with her there I don't have to think about what I'm doing. Usually I have to squeeze my eyes shut and try really hard to take my head to Jim or Disneyland or Taco Bell: all my someplace elses are far away from the lonely sweaty cars and it takes a lot of work to get to them. But with Tracy there the someplace else is right behind me, giggling, and she turns the whole thing into one big joke that we walk away from with lunch money.

That's how it is with the first three, at least; but the fourth one stops for her, not me. He's more than forty and he's got a mustache, which is always gross. I'm thinking he's not gonna be cool with me coming, but Tracy grabs me by the hand and pulls me in. His first question to her is "Who the hell is he?" He asks without even looking at me.

"He's my little brother; I'm just babysitting." She has this way of saying the most ridiculous things like they are completely one hundred percent normal, so normal you feel stupid arguing with her or even asking questions.

The guy just grunts and drives to an alley behind Lincoln. He puts the car in park and goes for her right away. I know I'm supposed to say funny things and distract Tracy like she does for me, but I can't think of anything to say. Also, I can tell this guy thinks I'm invisible and that's the only thing protecting me from getting my ass kicked. So I just slink down in the backseat as low as I can, and in my head I shrink smaller and smaller until I understand what people mean when they say "fly on the wall." From the back the only thing I can see is Tracy's face. She's looking out the windshield at nothing. Her eyes have that glassy tired mean look, and there's nothing I can do to make it funny or easier.

When it's over, she holds her hand out without looking at him. He sets the money on her palm like it's a table and I can tell he wants to say something but he doesn't. She opens the door and gets out onto the gravel.

I have to almost run to catch up with her. She's staring straight ahead with empty eyes; I'm afraid she's mad at me. But when I finally get beside her, panting, she snaps her eyes out of their stare and fills them up with herself again. "Hey," she goes, and pulls the money out of her pocket to show me. "Look, he gave me a tip."

"Cool," I say, still watching to make sure she's really here. She takes my hand and leads me toward the beach.

We go to the biggest food stand on the whole boardwalk, the one on the corner by Muscle Beach with yellow menus painted on the outside walls, and get pizza and onion rings and fries with extra ketchup and mayonnaise. Tracy buys an extra-large Coke for us too, and we take our food up to the hill by the sand and sit down on the thin cool grass and eat. If you look north you can see the curve of Malibu; the sunset silhouettes it, dark black mountains against the burning orange sky, and the pink ocean spread out in front of it forever, glistening and moving. If you look south it's all factories, some kind of chemical refinery: spidery towers stacked up all the way to the ocean, delicate and complicated as lace but ugly and stinky and made of hard metal. The smog browns the sunset and helicopters hover like big black bugs. While we eat, I turn my head back and forth a couple times, up at Malibu, down at Long Beach; I feel like a different person depending which direction I'm pointed. I finally settle on the mountains and finish the fries.

When we're done, I tell Tracy to take off her shoes and follow me north. We walk up the beach as the sun sinks and the sky turns purple, then gray, then black. By the time our feet get achy, we're almost up by Malibu; through Venice, past Santa Monica and the Vons by the highway pouring its late-night grocery-store light onto the sand. I've never been up this far before, but I know if you go much farther the beach starts being private property and you'll set off alarms just by walking. Here it's still free. We plop down on the sand, and right away Tracy lies back and starts counting stars. She only knows a couple. The waves crash in front of me and cars rush by in back, but the noise and moving feel really far away, like there's a cocoon of quiet and dark around us. After a long time she turns to me. "So where'd you come from, anyway?"

I realize we never talked about any of that: we were brother and sister from Fresno, it was all made up. "Bakersfield," I say.

"That's not too far," she goes. "What're you doing here?"

I start to say something but it stops in my throat like a plug. Jim made me promise not to tell and I haven't, not the whole two months I've been here waiting. That's what keeps me tied to him: the cords from me to Jim, from here to Bakersfield, are made up of a million little sparkling threads like spiderwebs; those threads are built from promises between us, the only thing that keeps me from floating away. If I tell our secret I know I'll cut those cords, and come untied, and I don't know where I'll go.

But Jim hasn't answered his phone in two months and I can't remember the sound of his voice. And Tracy is here, right here, and she is the only one who I could ever tell. And the night around us is quiet enough to keep a secret. So I do it. I tell her I am in love and I explain who Jim is and why I had to go, and that he said he's coming, but that he hasn't yet. I try to explain to her the feeling of locking together with someone like a puzzle piece, and it's not just your outsides that fit or the way you seem to the world, but all the inside parts of you that you didn't even know had a shape until they matched up so perfectly with his. Tracy's looking at me like she doesn't quite believe what I'm saying, like she's not sure it's possible for a person to feel that way with someone, and I understand: lots of people don't believe in love. And you have to believe in it before it will let you see or touch it, so if you don't make the leap you might not ever see it. But it's there.

Tracy doesn't know that. I can tell. But she asks me lots of questions, and it feels so good to answer. Jim's been more important to me than even myself for almost a year, and all of it has only happened in two places: inside of me or in the space between me and him. Telling Tracy's like opening a faucet.

It comes out of my mouth like water: the things he said at the beginning, what it's like to know a person's smell, the anxious catch that now has dulled to normal when I hold the pay phone and it rings and rings. How underneath I don't believe he's coming anymore, and I wish I could turn the air beside me into something solid to fill the hole he leaves. How sometimes when he'd touch me I'd go out onto the very edges of myself, far like on a tightrope or a plank, and balance knowing there was only air to catch me; how he'd hold me there till it got scary, sometimes longer, and it was realer and more raw than any thing I'd ever felt. How he would always close his eyes and seem so comfortable, casual even, and I was always amazed at that: how brave he must be for it not to scare him at all. How sometimes it broke me into two pieces, and I'd lie there under him naked and stretched out past my skin, and another me would watch from the ceiling. Even if it was too much I had to grow to hold it, because it belonged to me now, and I belonged to him, and if I let any of the pressure of it spill like water from my faucet mouth, it would all leak out and be gone from me forever. That's what he always said.

And he was right: now the words go out of me, and Tracy catches them, and somehow the swelling of the secrets shrinks down and Jim is smaller inside me, and far away. My own skin goes back to my own size finally and is tight enough to hold me; the space beside me is full of air and ocean and I'm all one piece. My cheeks are hot with tears, which run under my chin making it sticky, and I try to sniffle them up but they just keep coming, and I don't even know why, and Tracy takes my hand and holds it in the sand and we both watch the waves break, spreading out and getting sucked back into the sea.

We stay there all night, watching the red lights from the oil drills blink way out toward the sky. When the sun first starts to lift the curtain of black we finally fall asleep, just a little while before the cars start their early morning roar.

I wake up before Tracy does and lie there, watching. Everything looks different in daylight. I have this funny feeling in my chest, half light and half nervous, like I changed something big last night, even though all I did was talk.

I know Tracy didn't get the stuff I said about jigsaw puzzles and fitting together and love. But when I talked about the other stuff, the secret stuff—being stretched out past your edges, split in half, and the feeling you could fall and fall and nobody will ever let you tell—that was when she held my hand.

Something happened then: part of me that's been knotted up for a year came loose when I started telling all those things and Tracy heard me. Her fingers locked in mine, our palms pressed tight; we were together, but I could feel where she ended and I began. I never had that with a person ever: being close and whole at the same time. And I told her all the secret scary things, and the whole time she kept holding on to me.

I haven't showered in a month almost, but I feel clean. I lie there breathing and watch the nannies show up at the beach, all black and brown with other people's shiny white Malibu babies on their backs. They look at each other and laugh and are bored with the children and really, really tired. For some reason they make me think of me and Tracy working.

All of a sudden I want to get out of here. The beach is softer than the sidewalk in Hollywood and Tracy is my friend but our friendship is too much in the backs of guys' cars. I want to go back where no one knows that part of me.

Squid bought me a burrito just because he liked me. He didn't want anything back. My head fills up with his face and I need to get back to him.

I shake Tracy's shoulder. "Tracy," I whisper.

She rubs her eyes and looks up at me, bleary and soft. "Hey," she goes.

"I'm gonna catch the bus back in to Hollywood," I tell her. "You want anything before I go?"

She sits up and looks a way I've never seen her look: sad. "You're leaving?"

"Yeah, I gotta, uh—" and I don't know how to finish that sentence so I just scratch my head and look at the sand.

"Okay," she goes, louder, in her normal voice: sharp like broken glass, rough like cigarettes. "That's cool, man."

"Okay," I go.

"Okay," she goes again. I keep expecting her to say something more, but she doesn't; she just puts on her boots and starts lacing them up.

I stand up. "So I'll see ya." I don't want to say when, because I'm hoping to not have to come back.

"Okay," she goes. I walk over the hill of sand.

Staring out the gray-streaked bus window as the city rolls by, I realize I've been awake for two hours and haven't thought about Jim once. It's weird: I've been with Jim the whole time I've been a person; before that I was just a kid. And it's always been like in order to keep being myself I

75

have to be with him, or wait for him, or imagine him at least. And now I'm not. Instead I'm thinking about Tracy's face, and how it changes back and forth from hard to laughing, like she's going someplace else and coming back, and how I kind of recognize that back and forth even though I don't know why. I'm thinking that I have to find another way of making money, even though I'm not sure I really can. And I'm thinking about Squid. Inside my head I can see the exact shape of his cheek and where his freckles are, and there's something that folds up inside me, curled round and warm and right, when I think about Squid's face.

When I get off the 217 bus by Benito's, the three of them are right there, where they always are. It makes me feel like there's something I can count on. Germ sees me first and barks. Squid looks up and gets a big grin on his face and something twists inside me, in a good way even though it makes my legs feel wobbly. When I walk up Eeyore gives me a hug and Critter goes "Hey, man," and nods.

"Where'd you go, man?" Squid asks me, his face wide open.

I hadn't thought about having to explain. I freeze for a second, hold my breath and watch the traffic like I'm actually looking at something. "Uh—I went over to the beach," I say, and kick the sidewalk.

"Needed a little vacation, huh?" Critter says, and cracks a smile.

"Yeah," I breathe out. I meet his eyes: he can tell it's not the truth, but he isn't fucking with me either. "Yeah," I say again, relieved. And that's all anyone says about it.

That night when it gets dark, Critter and Eeyore go off to Dumpster for tomorrow. They're gone for a while, long enough for me and Squid to eat some tacos and for Squid to drink a 40 and get tired. When his eyes start to droop, we lie down in the alley by Benito's, heads on our backpacks. Some nightclub's got a searchlight and they're sweeping it against the sky, throwing up big beams that crisscross the black and drown out the stars. It makes me dizzy to look at it and I turn onto my side, away from Squid.

Even though I was up all last night with Tracy, I'm not tired. My whole body's awake, perked up like I'm nervous, except I'm not, not really. I watch the wall of the building beside us, count the bricks, try to stay quiet so Squid can fall asleep.

I've been lying there for fifteen minutes when I hear rustling behind me. I stay on my side, breathing, and listen to Squid move. There's more rustling and then I feel him near me, but not touching. He's close enough that I can feel his breath on my neck, just a little warmer than the hot night air. My heart starts pounding like a drum against the inside of my chest, so hard I'm sure he can hear it. I time my breaths so they're exactly even, faking sleep as perfectly as I can.

He doesn't move for about a minute. Eight breaths

exactly. Then he's up against me and I almost jump out of my skin, like when you're concentrating hard and someone suddenly talks. But I keep myself from moving and my eyes stay closed. My heartbeat's up in my head now, fluttering. Squid puts his arm around my waist and just stays there, pressed against me like spoons. His face brushes up against the back of my neck and I can feel his lips. I keep waiting for him to do something else, to want something from me, but he doesn't. We stay like that all night.

I sleep harder than I have since I came here. By the time I wake up the sun is high over our heads, spreading out in the sky, and Squid's a few feet away giving Germ water from a squeezy bottle. I wait a minute before I move too much or speak, so I'll have a chance to watch without him knowing. His shoulders are as wide and strong as two of me put together. His freckles are like a map across his cheeks.

After a minute I get nervous he'll see me looking, so I yawn loud, like I just woke up, and stretch my arms. He looks over at me. "Hey," he goes. "What's up."

"Morning," I go, and then wait. My heart starts thumping in my chest again. I guess I'm expecting him to say something about last night, or at least act different, but he just keeps giving water to Germ.

I guess I must be staring because after a minute he looks over and goes "What?" My whole body is hot and prickly but I say "Nothing."

He finishes with the dog and goes "I bet Critter and Eeyore are at Winchell's. Let's get some donuts," and gets up. Just like that. The whole way to Winchell's he doesn't say anything, and I feel like I'm keeping a big secret from him even though we both know the same things.

Since that night it's been different and almost exactly the same. Eeyore hangs on Critter's neck, and we four sleep back in the alleys and eat two-day-old donuts, and Squid sits with me to spange, and grins and buys me food when he's got cash. But he doesn't touch me again, and he never says anything about that night. I guess I feel like I can't either. Every day I spend beside Squid on the sidewalk I can feel my insides lock more into place with his, fitting up perfect like a brand-new puzzle, and so my secrets stretch out past my skin, out there unarmored in the hot air of Hollywood, and I don't want to point them out to him if he can't already see. I'm pretty sure it's not the same for him. Which means that there are lots of things I'll always have to never say.

But I still don't get how you can touch someone and act afterward like it didn't ever happen, like you're still just two separate people, the same safe pocket of air swelled up between you. When Squid and I are waiting for our food to come up at Benito's I watch him watch it cook and I think: I know what your breath feels like. I wonder if he ever thinks that about me.

squid

i *don't know how the fuck it got so noisy around* here. The last few weeks it seemed so quiet: with Critter here, plus Eeyore and Rusty, I finally was sleeping every night. Critter'd mumble stoned and drunk, Eeyore'd babble through her dreams, Rusty breathed out through his skinny chest and all of it was like a lullaby. But Critter and Eeyore left two days ago to unload junk, and when I came back today with breakfast Rusty wasn't there.

So tonight they're gone and I'm alone again and the less people there are around me the louder it all seems to get. Trucks drag by sounding like whole factories, creeping up then peaking and fading away, and I try to imagine they're waves crashing but the metal grinds against itself too hard for me to believe it's water. The hookers scream at each other half in Spanish, voices screechy like a girl's but loud and deep like guys. You can never tell if they're laughing or about to stab each other.

The sounds don't come and go; they add up, and

closing my eyes just makes it worse. In the inside of my head they turn into a million-petaled metal flower, or a herd of butterflies beating at the inside of my skull. I can feel every single cell of skin and hair on me, crawling. After a while the noise from outside doesn't even matter anymore: it's all inside. I count the stars to calm down, but they double up, start multiplying too. There's too many of everything everywhere and I can't keep track.

I get this feeling when I'm by myself too much.

Ever since I was a kid I had it. As far back as I can remember once my mom got too tweaked out to keep on running from my dad, and I started getting passed around to strangers. The feeling's like a rash. Right at the edge of my skin, except inside my mind.

Annabelle made it go away for a while, in Arizona and all the way out here. The quiet came from a place I didn't even know I remembered. I met her when we were both fifteen. I'd been floating around in foster homes for seven years and dropped out of school for two. She was reading fucking *Beowulf* for English. I fell right in love with her chopped-up hair and inky hands and faded bruises and made her skip class every day. It took ten months to get her to realize that if she ran away from her asshole dad and the leaky roof he kept above her head the world wouldn't end, it might even get better, but finally I did, and we took off on the trains. It was me and her and Germ in the open air, finding our own food and surviving. We even had plans.

But within a week of landing in L.A. Annabelle was headed up to Berkeley, following some stupid band she heard was there, and my head started roaring again.

Those first two weeks were pretty goddamn loud. When I met Critter underneath the 101 I stopped noticing the noise so much. First of all, just having another person's voice there drowned it out. And Critter always makes sure you eat, when he's around. He strolls down the Hollywood sidewalks like he's lived on them forever, and everybody knows him. It was nice having someone look out for me a little bit; I'd forgot what it felt like.

But Critter's just too fucking good-looking to be considered reliable, so things never really quieted down for real. Those four months that it was me and him it used to make me nervous: he's the kind of guy you might sometimes love but you don't really want to need, because he'll never ever need you back.

A month or so ago we found Eeyore back by the Dumpsters. Three days after that Rusty came along. Since then I was happier, and for the first time I could sleep: there's enough of us now that it's almost like a little family. Eeyore mostly only talks to Critter, but Rusty and me are perfect. He fits with what I'm missing somehow: our sentences match when we talk to each other. That never happened to me with anyone except Annabelle. I thought you only got it once per life until I bought Rusty some burritos and we started talking. I mean, he's not a girl, so I guess it's different that way. But he needs me and that part's the same.

But now Rusty's gone and he didn't say where he was going. I know he's not used to being out here, and I didn't think he was the type to just leave. I've been wondering what he's gonna eat since this morning. How he'll find his way back here, no bread crumbs. And I keep trying to keep track of everything I did and said, in case I made him go away by accident. I can't stop. I lean over into Germ and listen to him snore, hoping it'll drown out all the other noise. At least Germ's not going anywhere. Nobody's gonna feed him but me.

Of course right when I finally get to sleep, the sun comes up. I roll over into my backpack to stretch out the dark, but one sound gets in, and then another and another, and I'm up. I keep my eyes shut anyway. Against the black-eyelid backdrop my mind picks up where it stopped last night, keeping track. I'm not worried about Critter: he's always leaving to buy shit or sell it, and he always comes back. I know Eeyore went with Critter because that's what she does, and she'll be back when he's back for the same exact reason. But that still leaves Rusty.

The light gets brighter and brighter through my eyelids while I lie there till everything looks blank and red. Halfway into rush hour Germ hears something near us. He picks up his head. His collars clink together before the leash tugs on my hand; then he's up and jumping, happy; shitty watchdog. I open my eyes and he pulls me with him: slobbers his face into the bag Eeyore's holding, rustling the grease-stained white till Critter grabs it away from both of them, takes a glazed donut and gives it to Germ. Critter slaps my hand hi. Eeyore copies his smile. They're back.

Their voices take the edge off my alone—at least I've got something else to listen to—but after hello they mostly talk to each other, as usual. Nobody needs anything from me. I could turn invisible and they probably wouldn't notice. I pick at the sole of my boot and talk to Germ. Rusty's still gone. I spend the next two hours wondering if he's coming back.

At ten the 217 bus pulls up and I get my answer. He's the fourth one out the door, after two Mexican guys and an old white lady who looks like she's made out of dust. He seems nervous in a happy way, the way I guess you're supposed to be before the first day of school, or prom, or whatever shit you're supposed to do if your mom's not a tweaker and your dad didn't beat her up and you live in a house instead of on the sidewalk. When I see his face my insides finally start to settle and the wings in my head slow down. It's still loud in there but his face helps, his nose and eyes. He stutters up to us like he wants to run and he's making his feet slow down. I wish he'd hurry up.

That night in the alley I get up close enough to him that the breathing sounds drown out the hookers and the trucks. I wrap my arms around him so he can't leave again. My head is just one thing, quiet now, and I can get to sleep.

I think something happened with Critter and Eeyore while they were off selling that shit. All last night and today he's been keeping her really close but distant at the same time. You can tell that he's preoccupied, like a dad on TV who's got something on his mind. He doesn't say what, though. They never do on TV either.

Critter never says what's on his mind, but usually he at least says other things instead. Usually he says "Come here" to everyone and smokes us up, or buys us dinner. Always making sure that no one's hungry. He smiles with those movie-star eyes and laughs about something and makes you feel like out here's the best and freest place to be, even if you're only here to run away from somewhere else. Eeyore went right to it like a moth to a lightbulb, the hot glass of him the only bright space in the dark. She hasn't left him since.

But now Critter won't talk, and I can tell Eeyore's lonely. I wish I could take care of her. I like taking care of things that are smaller than me. They remind me of myself a long time ago, I guess. There's nothing I can do, though; Eeyore won't let me. She'd rather hide under piles of bravado or else nestle under Critter's arm like a baby bird. Even when he hardly moves to let her in. I want to tell her to quit it: he could pull out from under any time. That's what guys like him do, guys like dads on TV who feed everyone and give you drugs and never admit that they need anything. But they always seem like the strongest of all if you don't know better. And she doesn't.

Now Critter comes up to us from the Goodwill parking lot, holding on to Eeyore like her arm's a leash, and plops her down. She scowls.

"Would you take care of her for a while, guys? I gotta go pick up some shit," Critter goes. I'm glad to but Eeyore looks pissed: this is obviously the middle of something that started already.

"What the fuck, Critter?" Eeyore says. "I *told* you I want to come." She lets it hang there for a second, but he doesn't bite. "C'mon, I won't fuck anything up, I promise, you can say I'm your little sister—" she's begging now. But Critter's got his mind made up, he's not hearing any arguments.

"I told you, Juan-Carlo's got his eye on you, he thinks you're worth money and I'm not taking you back there."

Eeyore rolls her eyes. "I don't even know what you're *talking* about. You are so paranoid. All he said is I was cute. That's a *compliment*."

Critter just looks at us like we all understand what Eeyore doesn't, which we do. "Sure," I go, "she can hang out with us," and she scowls again. This time at me.

"Thanks," Critter says, then throws a half-empty bag of

Doritos down at us. "That's for her," he goes. Germ scuttles over to sniff it.

Eeyore is pissy for the next seven hours. It's obvious she's mad because of Critter. He's trying to protect her, but there's no way I can say that: I'd rather have her mad at him than me. It gets to where I want to get her drunk just to take the edge off, and I don't usually feel that way. I'm getting nervous she'll blow up and leave, or Rusty will, or someone. Finally I have to do something, so I buy us a 40, most of which Eeyore downs almost immediately. We go walking. If I take us somewhere better maybe it'll help.

On Formosa there's this huge construction site. I don't know what they're building there, a high-rise or a mini-mall, but they've been digging for three months and nothing's come up but dust and piles of steel. We pass by it sometimes on the way to Whole Foods, the wood walls with the "warning" signs and construction trucks like dinosaurs grumbling around inside. Fluorescents shine down on it like helicopter searchlights but I don't care. I hand Eeyore Germ's leash, tell Rusty to give me a boost and slide up the wall, flip over the edge and scrape my stomach on the other side.

Once I'm over, the two of them don't really have any choice but to follow. Rusty lifts Germ all the way up. I can tell Rusty's on his tiptoes because all you can see is Germ teetering from side to side, scrambling like a little pig. I hold my arms up to Germ. He trusts me like always, and I catch him. Then there's a pause for a second before Eeyore's pink face peeks past the edge. I wave at her: *Come on*. For a second she looks scared, like the weak kid in dodgeball who's about to get hit. Then Rusty hoists her up and over and she lands in the red dirt next to me.

When Rusty gets stuck at the top, I reach up and pull him the rest of the way. He lands on his knees, stands quick to brush them off. I ask if he's all right. He doesn't say anything, just looks up like he's glad to be on the same side of the wall as us.

Eeyore is officially almost drunk. Plus she's excited I think, so she forgets her bad mood and turns cute like a kid. She runs around the edge of the enormous crater pit that the construction dinosaurs dug. It goes down a hundred feet, like the top of a volcano, except there's no fire at the bottom, just more dirt. Around the edges of the pit, piles of steel beams and wood planks make mountains on the ground, and the yellow and orange creature machines sleep standing up. The wood walls shut out the light from the street. It's black, except where the work lights shine down like a stadium, and then it's so bright you can hardly look at it. It's beautiful. I look at Eeyore and Rusty, both grinning. It worked. I brought them someplace better.

Eeyore stumbles us across the site like we're astronauts, climbing over hills of lumber, darting in and out of light. For a minute we can't see her. Then her little voice yells

"Guys!" We run up. She's standing in front of a shack, three-quarters built. It's dark-green painted wood and flimsy metal. The floor is dust. There are little windows with no glass in them and a door frame with no door. Eeyore shrieks like she found a gingerbread house in the woods; runs into it and sits right down. Rusty and I go in after.

Inside the light filters through the little window holes. None of us are used to being inside anywhere that's ours. It's usually either out in open air or in some store that someone owns. And I guess somebody owns this too, but it doesn't feel like it. The sounds from the sidewalks barely even get in here. Rusty and I grin at each other, trying to hear the quiet.

Eeyore's drunk, though, so she starts jabbering. It stirs up the air, but nobody minds. She's happy talking. Mostly we just listen: Critter the asshole should've let her go with him, don't we think so, come on guys (we nod). Man. He always lets her come, she's never messed it up; Juan-Carlo'd give Critter a deal if she was there. She really thinks Juan-Carlo likes her.

Rusty and I just look at each other when she says that. It's not funny, but for some reason the look in Rusty's eyes makes me laugh sudden like a sneeze, too fast for me to stop it coming out. Rusty laughs back, like a reflex. Then it wears off and he looks away from me. I stop laughing too. I look at Eeyore for a second. I see her eyes fill up.

"Shit, man," I say to her. "I didn't mean anything—"

"What the fuck are you laughing about?" she goes, in

that choky way you talk when you're trying to get words out past tears. I can't really answer. I guess we were laughing because Juan-Carlo likes her in a different way from how she thinks, but that's not funny, it's more scary if you think about it. Plus I don't think she'd believe me if I told her that; I think she'd just get mad. So I just say "Nothing." Which only makes her madder.

"Fuck you, Squid," she goes. "You guys always fucking laugh at me behind my back. Don't think I don't notice," but it's really actually not true, it's really the first time it's ever happened, and it wasn't behind her back it was actually right in front of her face, so I go "What are you talking about? Are you crazy or something?" which comes out a little harsher than I meant it, and then I think I must've snorted, because she gets like ten times louder and yells "Don't fucking laugh at me!" like she's a three-year-old trying to stop a grown-up from leaving, squeezing her eyes shut, using every last inch of vocal cord she's got plus all her muscles, like it'll actually make a difference. Rusty slouches down like he wants to be invisible.

I start to open my mouth, but she's yelling now. She's not gonna stop. "I'm not fucking crazy! I know you all think I'm a loser and I'm not enough of a hardass to hang out with you and I'm sorry my dad didn't beat me up when I was five or whatever, but I have problems too, you know." My heart starts speeding up and I try to talk again but she just keeps going, snot running out of her nose all over her upper lip.

She's freaking out. "I've had shit happen that you guys have no fucking idea about, okay? You know what? You don't know what it feels like to be molested by your fucking step-brother every fucking night of your life. You don't know what that shit feels like. So fuck you. Fuck you." The last "fuck you" she kind of chokes on. And then she puts her head down on her knees and says "Get away from me" into her sleeve.

I've got that worried rash feeling on my skin again. I'm sweaty from getting yelled at; my heart's beating hard in my ears. I must've done something bad to make her feel like that. It must've been bad when I laughed. I don't want to be that guy, the one that laughs at kids and hurts their feelings, but somehow it wound up that way and I don't know how to undo it. I'm sure Rusty thinks I'm a huge asshole. He still won't look at me. Eeyore will, but her shiny eyes are like a mirror. I'm afraid to look at them.

I want to do what she said, just get up and get away from her and go, but I can't leave her and Rusty here. They wouldn't know how to get back without me. So I just go, "You know what? Fuck you, Eeyore."

I don't even know why. It's not really what I mean. I just want to push her away because she makes me feel so bad. I hear the edge in my voice when I say it: I remind myself of someone else, although I'm not sure who.

Rusty looks up at me then, with this look I can't quite read, half disappointed and half scared. Like I suddenly have someone else's face. "Squid?"—he says it like a question.

"What?" I go. My voice sounds hard and sudden. He flinches. Then he doesn't talk.

"*What?*" I go again. I can't stand not knowing what he's going to say. His mouth stays shut. He looks like he just got busted and doesn't have an explanation for it. But I want to make him give me one. I keep staring at him.

Finally he just says "Nothing. It's cool, man." It sounds weird in his mouth, like he really wants to say something else. I can't tell what, though. Then he looks at Eeyore, then at me. "Right?"

After a minute I go "Yeah, I guess." Eeyore's still got snot on her lip, but she doesn't say anything. Germ flops over on his side. No one talks. I lie down next to Germ, my back to them, and listen to him pant. After a second Rusty and Eeyore lie down too, first him, then her. My eyes are closed but I hear them. I keep my eyes shut, slow my breath so they'll think I'm asleep and the whole thing can be over. That noisy itchy feeling starts to creep up inside again, even though I'm not even by myself, not really. The car sounds outside layer on top of each other, building, and I brace myself for another night awake. I must be tired, though: before the noise can take over I pass out.

I'm awake already when the dark starts to lift. Little streams of light leak in through the cracks in the wood of the shack.

The windows make squares on the ground; dust swirls around inside them. I lean in and shake Rusty's shoulder. He opens his eyes right at me, surprised to see my face so close. He blinks twice and then looks at me normal. "Hey," he goes, and smiles a little. I can tell there's nothing else he wants to say instead. My heart's been high up near my throat since last night, but now it settles back into the right place in my chest. Rusty glances over at Eeyore, who's still sleeping on the red dirt floor. She looks like a little kid, curled up on her side, one hand up by her mouth and one between her knees. "Do you think she's okay?" Rusty whispers.

"Yeah," I say, because I don't really know any other answer.

By the time it's bright out I've bought everybody breakfast. We even went to Jack in the Box, which costs way more than donuts. It took me down to the last fifty cents I panhandled this week, but I wanted to make sure everyone knows I'm not an asshole. At the register Rusty went digging in his sock. I saw he had some cash wadded there, but I told him to quit it. Eeyore just took the food without looking at me and her cheeks turned red.

When we get back to Benito's Critter's already there, squatted down on the parking lot curb. He's with this other guy. The guy's probably seventeen and he's that kind of redhead whose eyelashes and eyebrows are all orange too, freckles blanketing his face and arms over the sunburn. He's wearing black patched-up Carhartts and a bull ring through his nose. His T-shirt says *Crass*. He's fiddling with the hardware knotted into his crusty red dreadlocks, steel rings and black rubber and nuts without the bolts, and he won't look at us. I can tell he's mean. Critter's pissy too, in some mood about something. The two of them just sit there in that mood like it's a couch.

I have to walk right up to the guy and stare him down before he'll even look at us. "Hey," I go. "I'm Squid." And he doesn't even talk, just raises his eyebrows like there's something I'm supposed to do. I don't do anything. Finally Critter says "I know Scabius from back in Reno. I ran into him on Hollywood this morning."

Rusty slouches back behind my shoulder, chewing on his hand. At first Eeyore does too, and it's like there's two little groups, them on the curb and the three of us standing. I spread out my shoulders so there's room back there for Eeyore and Rusty both. Eeyore stays back there. For a minute I think maybe she might be okay with me again.

But then she darts out and squats down by Critter on the curb. Even though he seems mad, way madder than yesterday, and even though Scabius is coiled beside him like a guard dog, she goes right back to Critter. I know she's got a crush on him, but it still makes me feel bad. Like even Critter pissed off, with some weird guy, is better than me buying breakfast.

As soon as Eeyore sits down he starts swearing: Juan-

Carlo stiffed him last night, took all his money but didn't give him his drugs. Eeyore looks over at Scabius and starts to say something about how if she was there Juan-Carlo wouldn't have done that, but Critter's eyes flash hard and it makes her shut up. She scrunches up her shoulders and leans away but watches from the side, like Germ does with me when he's in trouble. She knows not to push it any further once she gets caught. All she can do is try and make herself invisible so he won't turn it on her.

It's obviously not the first time Scabius has heard the story of Juan-Carlo. He doesn't say anything, but you can feel him backing Critter up, feeding it. Critter swears some more and then finally jumps up and starts tearing around the parking lot, like water that was heating up and heating up and all of a sudden boiled. He throws his backpack down, yells how he's got nothing left now. His face is pink, like in a movie when the main guy gets mad and hurls a chair against a wall. And it's a pretty noisy show he's putting on, but I can tell he's sort of acting. Half of him is actually mad, but the other half is doing it on purpose. Part of him has got the whole thing under control. If he was really all that angry, my stomach would crawl and my head would get noisy and I'd feel that hit-dog thing that Eeyore did. And I don't.

The hookers turn their heads to watch; the tallest one in leopard print and purple shoes puts her hand in her purse, and a guy parking his BMW nearby looks nervous. Critter notices the guy and gets louder. I think I know why he's pretending to be the mad guy in the movie. I can guess what he's thinking: if he freaks out loud enough, one of us will offer to put up cash so he can buy another round of shit to sell. Just asking would be a whole lot easier, but guys like Critter never think anyone will give them anything unless we're scared.

I'd help him, maybe, but I'm tapped out after Jack in the Box. He's not going to get much from anyone else here either, I don't think. Eeyore never has money, even though she can always find food. Rusty's clutching his sock from the side, and I know what's inside it but he's not talking. And Scabius doesn't seem the type to help anyone out with anything. He just watches all of us like a wolf figuring out where everyone is in the pack.

Critter bounces back toward us, his face red, breathing heavy. "Fuck," he goes and collapses, acting like he's giving up so one of us will tell him not to.

Eeyore's watching him. She's not hunching like a scolded dog anymore. She's standing up. All of a sudden. "Come on," she says to him. "Let's go back to my house. I've got money there."

Of course that stops everything. "You have a *house*?" Critter asks her.

She stammers a little, pulls back, quits standing up so straight. "Well, it's not *my* fucking house," she says, throwing the *fucking* in to make sure she sounds tough. "It's my stepmom's. And my dad's."

"They live here?" Critter goes. Eeyore nods. "Fuck," Critter says. There's a minute where we all look at each other: it's a little fucking weird that Eeyore has a house, especially one she can go back to. It sort of makes her not exactly one of us. And we all know it. And it looks like Eeyore just figured it out too. And there's this long pause. Then Critter looks at Scabius and goes "Well, I'm not going to anybody's fucking *house*."

Eeyore gets this look like she wants to reach out into the air in front of her mouth and swallow it all, like she wants to take back time, but she knows she can't and so she's frozen there, panicked. Her mouth moves a little but she doesn't say anything. It hardly looks like she's breathing. I wonder if she's going to cry.

I say, "I'll go with you."

Critter's still pink in the face and he throws a little of it in my direction. Scabius catches it and copycats, shooting me a scowl like an echo. I don't mind, though. I know Critter had to say he wasn't going and stick to it, just like I have to say I'll go. I peek over at Rusty: that look he had in the shack last night, the half-disappointed and half-nervous one, is all gone now, and now his face is something more like admiration. I hand him Germ's leash.

"Here," I go. "Will you watch him?" I never leave Germ with anyone. But right now I know he'll be okay with Rusty. And I know Germ'll look out for Rusty too.

I pet Germ on the head and leave his water bottle. I say

to Eeyore "Come on." Her face is still half frozen and I know she wants to hate me, except that I just saved her ass.

Eeyore and I walk up Vine until the street narrows and the fast-food places turn into expensive coffee shops. Then grocery stores, and then just hills. After a while there aren't any sidewalks so we walk in the street. We pass the Scientology Celebrity Centre that looks like a country club from the outside or a fancy hotel, green hard hedges flat and tall, high enough to keep out the people like us. The guards in their weird old-fashioned uniforms glare at us with blank eyes, white marble pillars tucked behind them. The whole time we've been gone, Eeyore hasn't said anything to me.

To tell you the truth, I'm happy to not talk to her. I still don't know how to explain last night. It still feels weird and knotted up in my chest like hair in a drain, and the best I can do to rinse it out is come with her and let her lead the way. I don't know how to do any better than that. Even though it's probably not enough.

She keeps seeming like she wants to say something, looking over in my direction and then down at asphalt or out at palm trees and parking lots. I can see when she's looking at me, but I pretend I can't. I'm like Annabelle right before she left for Berkeley: I knew she knew when I was looking at her, even though she pretended not to. I used to hate that. And now I'm doing it. It's funny how easy it is to do the things you hate, the things you promise yourself you'll never do. You look at grown-ups, tucked into their falling-apart houses, lying till they hit each other and you say you'll never be like that but who knows? It's easier than you think.

It just happens. Even when almost everyone who showed you how to do things showed you wrong, and screwed you up, and left; even when you have promised yourself in fifteen different sets of sheets and in freight trains and on sidewalks, staring up at stars, that you will do it different from all the people who have done it wrong and hurt you, still you do it the same. Still you do the same shit to everybody else that they have done to you. I know it must be possible to keep promises. There must be people who say things and mean them and who can make the words turn real. But I've never met one. I keep trying to be something I'm not even sure exists. I've promised myself so many times that I won't be like so many people, and I still do it anyway. I still make people cry, and laugh at them, and I know as soon as everyone really sees me they'll all leave again and I'll be left with the noise not being able to sleep.

The clouds are graying the sky and we're up at the top of a hill. You can see the smog blanket and the blinking canyon of Los Angeles below. My legs hurt. Eeyore steers us through a gateway into a corridor of flowers, hot pink and orange with the petals shaped like leaves. It's weird how L.A. is a city but once you get into rich people's yards it's like you're in a crazy jungle forest made of flowers. You can hardly see the house.

I follow her up to the front door. She already looked in the driveway. There's no car, so she doesn't try to be quiet. She digs under a flowerpot for the key. I make a note in my head where it is, even though I know I'll never come back and steal from here without her. Habit, I guess.

She doesn't seem embarrassed that we're here. In front of Critter she felt like a loser even saying she had parents, worried he would think she wasn't cool. She has no idea probably that he's just jealous. Now she's puffed up and brave-acting, like kids who break into houses in movies. All tough shoulder swagger, one hand in her magenta hair. Her other hand shakes gripping the key in the lock.

She wiggles it open anyway, though, and it creaks. We go into the front hall which is covered in beige carpet, so clean it's almost shiny. We both get boot prints on it. I tell her sorry and bend down to rub mine out with my shirt: I've stolen enough to know you don't leave tracks. But she just goes "It's cool, man" and motions me back up before I'm done. I let her be in charge, even though I know it's not a good idea. It's funny how she acts like Critter when he's not around.

She says "Come on" and heads upstairs to the living room. I've never been inside a house like this. Some of my fosters had money, but just the small-town-in-Arizona kind, never like people in big cities have. The best I've seen is stucco ceilings, little wooden tables, and a comfortable plaid couch. Mostly the houses I've been in have holes in the walls. But this one has fancy peach paint and a big leather couch and a TV that's stretched out flat like a movie screen. Part of the floor is cold gray marble and the other part is wood, and lights hang from the ceiling like the kind you see through windows inside fancy restaurants. There are even miniature palm trees growing inside in pots. I feel like I'm in a TV show.

Eeyore goes to the kitchen. The refrigerator is huge and shiny silver. She grabs my backpack off my back and starts stuffing it. Peanut butter, hummus, juice. She's taking so much I get scared someone will notice, but when I look in the refrigerator it's still packed so full that you can't really tell. I know she's still mad at me from yesterday: she hasn't talked to me except to tell me what to do and where to go. The more she takes, though, the happier she seems. She's proud, I think, is what it is.

Between jars clinking in the fridge there's a clunk from down the hall. She doesn't stop until I put my hand on her wrist, my breathing slowed way down, and tell her "Shhh." She slides some cheese into my bag and stops to listen. My ears are like a rabbit.

There's another clunk. And then a doorknob twisting, and then footsteps. "Shit," I whisper. I look for windows we can climb out of. There aren't any; all of them have screens. The feet get fast and louder.

Then they come into the kitchen. I guess the lady's Eeyore's mom, even though she doesn't look a thing like her. She's in a business suit and panty hose, no shoes, like she was taking a nap in the middle of work. Her brown hair is blow-dried and she's pretty in that brittle sort of way. Her eyes go wide open when she sees us.

She looks at Eeyore: her face crumples up like she's about to cry, and she yells "Elly!" She starts to run to her, tears spilling out. But then she looks at me.

Her eyes narrow into little slits. I've gotten that face before, but usually from cops. I follow her gaze down onto my shirt and shorts and boots. I watch as her lip curls at the dirt. There's almost as much on her own kid's clothes, but she can't see it. All she can see is me. I watch it take five seconds for a story to click into place: for everything to become my fault inside her head. Then she turns right back to Eeyore.

"Is this what you ran away to be with?" she says. Like it's hardly a question, like I'm hardly a person. She's giving Eeyore that slit-eyed cop look now.

"No," Eeyore goes, like *Duh*, and makes a face like *That was the stupidest question on earth*. Her mom doesn't buy it. She turns back to me.

"How old are you?"

"Sixteen," I tell her.

"Do you know how old Elly is?" she asks me.

"Thirteen?" I guess.

102

"Twelve. She's twelve years old. You have taken a twelve-year-old out of her house and put her in God knows what kind of danger. I don't know who you are or what you think you are doing, but you are not going to do it with my daughter."

"I'm not your daughter," Eeyore mutters.

The woman flips around. *"What?"*

"You're not my fucking mom, Linda," Eeyore says. Her voice is quiet and mad.

It's obviously true, because it stops Linda for a second. But just a second: "You know what, young lady? I don't care. I'm tired of you raking me over the coals because I'm not your mother. I've had it. Your father and I work ourselves to the bone to give you *everything*. And then you run off with—" She can't even say it; she just looks at me. When I look back her eyes ricochet right off my face and land on Eeyore.

"You don't give me anything," Eeyore says. She's angry like the cherry of a cigarette, but also small, and scared. Everyone else in the room is bigger than her, could rub her out beneath our shoes.

"Aside, of course, from the food you're stealing from my refrigerator. That's it. You're staying here, and this"— she looks at me like she doesn't know what to call me, like she wants to spit—"*boy* is leaving. Right. Now."

I've got no objections to leaving. In fact, I'd like to do it immediately. But I can see on Eeyore's face that she can't stay. And I remember from last night the reason why.

There's a face-off. Eeyore just stands there, silent. Her body's like steel but her face is trembling. I can see tears start to well up in her eyes. I know once they spill out it'll be over: she'll crumble and stay. Eeyore is little and Linda is bigger and Critter's not here for Eeyore to run to and I've been in enough bad houses to know what it means if she stays.

"She's leaving." I hear myself say it: my heart's loud in my ears like last night and blood runs fast into my fingertips.

Both of them turn to look at me. Linda's still in charge: she squints at me like I'm a bug she wants to step on. I try again, louder—"She doesn't want to stay with you"—and before I can even finish the words she's yelling at me. She says "Get out" and "I'm calling the police." But she doesn't make a move for the phone.

"Fuck you," I tell her, just to call her bluff. Then her eyes flash and she's angry, all of her, not half of her like Critter in the parking lot. She calls me a bunch of names, lips curled, flecks of spit flying out of her mouth. Dirty, ugly, criminal. I recognize the words: they jolt me back inside my ears to a place that's familiar and old. Now she doesn't sound like cops. She sounds like a way-back feeling inside my ribs, and her words tunnel around me in the kitchen. All I can see is right in front of my eyes and everything goes clear like glass and I feel weirdly calm. Linda finishes with "—she ran away to be with filth like you." I didn't even hear what came before that, but I know what to tell her.

"No she didn't." I notice Eeyore's watching me, but I can't tell what her eyes look like. "You want to know why she ran away?" I think Eeyore might be crying. "She ran away because your kid, whatever the fuck his name is, was raping her for fucking years. Did you know that? Did you do anything? Probably fucking not. So don't blame me that Eeyore ran away. She ran away from you." My face is hot and when the words are done I notice that I'm panting.

She just stands there like an idiot. Her mouth is a little open, like she's sleeping in a chair. Eeyore's not moving, except for her face: she's definitely crying for real now. Snot and tears mix on her chin. I watch her out of the corners of my eyes. She looks at me to see what I'll do next; I keep my eyes on Linda.

Linda reminds me of a cow, heavy and blank. Like if you tipped her over she wouldn't know how to get back up.

She doesn't say anything. It's just a few seconds but it seems like forever. The silence swells up the room. I glance over and Eeyore's face is like a little kid's, wide open, waiting. All her street-kid bluster is gone and she's staring at Linda, stripped down to a place I haven't felt since I was five, so soft I wouldn't be surprised if she stretched out her arms and asked to be picked up.

"You're lying," Linda says. She says it to me but then she looks at Eeyore, testing her out. Eeyore doesn't talk— she can't, I think—but after a second she shakes her head, just an inch, the smallest, softest answer she can give.

Linda's voice gets louder now, hard and strong like a boss at work. "You're lying," she says again, this time to Eeyore.

It's like a door slides across Eeyore's face and slams shut hard enough to lock itself. Her mouth stitches up and her jaw clamps down. The only thing left from before are her eyes, wet and warm. That feeling of wanting to take care of her swells up in the middle of my chest, pressing against a hot fierce kind of mad that comes from farther below.

Sometimes Germ'll go nuts like a watchdog when some random guy walks too close on the sidewalk, barking and whining and jumping around. That's never when I worry. When someone's really dangerous he lets out this slow growl, too soft for anyone to hear except for who it's meant for. "She's not lying," I say to Linda. It comes out quiet and low.

Her voice just gets higher. "She's my daughter, I should damned well know when she's lying." I want to remind her that Eeyore's not her daughter, but she just keeps going. "You think you know better than her own family?" and points laser eyes at me.

"Yeah, I do," I say. It's not a fight, it's just true.

She can't really say anything back to that, so she starts talking to me like I'm five. Her voice turns singsong like nursery school except there's metal behind it. "Okay, I'm going to explain this to you, even though I know you're not going to understand. Eleanor is a rebellious teenager. She has to hate her parents. And you've obviously brainwashed her into thinking that you and whatever the hell you do are a lot more fun than living with us and going to school. We're a good, healthy, happy family here, so in order to run off with you, Eleanor has to invent a problem. That's what's going on. Eleanor is lying, and you believe her lies; or maybe you came up with them in the first place, I don't know. But I'm the adult here. My job is to protect her. And protecting her means getting her away from you."

"It does not!" Eeyore yells. It breaks the lock Linda and I have on each other. We both turn around. Eeyore's face is pink and her feet are stomped down. Her eyes are bright and mad. "Squid and Critter and Rusty take care of me. You don't. You don't fucking do anything. All you care about is your job and my dad and stupid Brian, and you do anything any of them tells you to and you don't give a shit about me. You just pretend you do so my dad will like you. You're a liar. You don't give a shit about protecting me. If you did you would believe me."

Eeyore stops there, almost surprised that last part came out of her mouth. She stares at Linda, chin still tilted up, feet still planted. Linda stares back until she can't. She stammers and her eyes brush the floor for a second. Then she points them up at me and opens her mouth to start in. I'm an easier target.

Before she can think of what to say, I shrug. "She's right," I tell Linda. "If you were protecting her you'd believe her."

And then I turn around to Eeyore and I say "Wanna go?" and she looks at me with the surest eyes in the world and says "Yeah." I grab her backpack and she grabs my hand, and we turn and go downstairs and out the door, headed back toward Winchell's and Benito's and our little sidewalk family. Linda doesn't try to stop us. On the way out Eeyore stops to put the key back. Then she changes her mind and pockets it.

scabius

"**W**hen the shit finally goes down we're gonna be the cockroaches," I tell Critter, and he grins at me with his gnarly chipped tooth and passes me the 40. "Shut the fuck up, man," he says, but I know he knows it's true. We're the toughest motherfuckers in this silicone Babylon, and when all the yuppies finally melt down in their PT Cruisers, soft as wadded-up tissues and just as fuckin' flammable, we'll still be here to live off their burnt-up waste. We already know how.

He's always busting my balls when I talk about the way it's all laid out, what's coming down, but I don't give a shit. We're on the same page. Like: here we are spare-changing up on Hollywood by the Ripley's museum and the parasites have been passing us by for three hours with their "get-a-job" fat tourist shit, and I know Critter hasn't eaten in more than half a day but he gets up to take a piss and comes back with a Dumpstered slice of pepperoni, all intact, no mold, and hands it over to *me*. I'd tell him thanks but he already knows so I just say "You fucker" and offer him the crust.

Altogether I've known Critter ten months and two cities, which out here is going on forever. When I met him in Reno I'd been there three weeks and knew I wasn't staying: Tahoe tourists could suck my dick and plus it was summer, so no guilty college kids to drop their quarters in your cup. I'd hitched from Cedar City, Utah, a.k.a. "home," a.k.a. Hell; finally ran for good when my drunk-ass dad knocked out three of my teeth and went for his gun. I was used to the blood in my mouth: we'd been cooped up in that rusty trailer since Mom took off when I was eight. But the gun was new.

I was planning on Vegas but a ride north on 15 came first, so Salt Lake for half a year, then west on 80, and before I knew it I was stuck in scenic Reno, old-fart vacation paradise. Everyone in pastels getting ready to die, and I was out of cash. Critter came up on me spare-changing by the A&W, sat down, and told me fuck all of fuckin' Nevada. He'd come out there following some girl who'd since fucked some guy and now he was homesick as shit for L.A. I told him fuck that girl. When he took off he lent me five bucks and told me I could pay him back in Hollywood.

Next time I saw him was at Benito's on Santa Monica. I bought him five rolled tacos for $2.99. I still owed him two more bucks, but he said he wasn't thirsty.

In Hollywood you can see it coming better than just about anywhere. Back in Utah everyone's always talking about the end times, battening down their hatches, but they don't really know. They can stockpile all the Costco shit they want, build chicken-wire compounds for their sixty wives out in the orange dust desert and pray to their big daddy God, but when the shit hits the fan they'll be lost without Wal-Mart. It's all a big bedtime story to them anyway. But in L.A. you can see it. Stretch Humvees with blue neon on the bottom, mansions big as Marriotts, the same twenty faces pasted on seven hundred billboards posters magazines: they narrow down what you can look at till the parts of your brain that know how to survive shrivel up and you're left driving from Staples to Rite Aid to Vons, feeling really fuckin' concerned about Cameron Diaz's love life. I mean, not that I'm not concerned with Cameron Diaz's love life. I could maybe help her out with that. But you know what I mean.

I don't look at billboards. No airbrushing for me. The L.A. I live in is the same now as it will be afterward: alleys, underpasses, Dumpsters, trash. Smashed glass, crumbled concrete, holes in fences. It's all about finding the cracks in things and shoving them open till they're big enough for you to squeeze in. That's where Critter and me crash most nights, in between buildings or up against cars, practicing, I guess, for when the whole world is roofless.

We were wedged between the 7-Eleven and a chain-link fence the night that Mr. Drunkfuck came to steal my shit. Critter and me'd been hanging out a week by then but only from convenience: there wasn't anything about it that was realer than just being in the same spot as each other every day. I sort of tacked on to Critter's crew: Rusty, Squid and Germ, this little chick called Eeyore who couldn't've been more than twelve but had tits already and burgundy hair like a two-day-old bruise. Eeyore'd hang around and spange for us, buy us 7-Eleven hot dogs, extra relish. She had some home to go to when she wanted: she'd leave sometimes in the afternoons, come back before five smelling like warm food and detergent, but she was all right. The mascot, kinda.

Anyway the night of Drunkfuck it must've been five in the morning because the sky was halfway between dark and light, still blue like a pair of clean jeans with no smog or sun to yellow it, sunrise creeping up from underneath. This fucker came up the alley yelling "Eeyore," sounding like a donkey, waking us all up. I could taste the Mad Dog from last night in the spit-strings between my lips, and I smelled the same shit coming off of Mr. Drunk except he had a fresh bottle in his hand at five in the morning; plus he was at least forty, so he had no excuse. A beard, too. One of those guys.

He slurred, tipping sideways like a top that just stopped spinning, "Eeyore said she'd buy me breakfast." Critter and Squid sat up, rubbing their eyes; Germ perked his ears up and Rusty rolled over. Eeyore must've woken up early, gone for donuts. "Where'z she go?"

Squid laid back down on his pack, closed his eyes

halfway: good-bye, Mr. Drunkfuck. But the guy kept on talking: she promised she'd be here to buy him eggs and he was hungry, man, and what was he supposed to do. Fuckin' Eeyore. She was always talking to losers like this, thinking she could make them her friends. Something about the smell of his breath pissed me off, even though mine probably stank the same, and I looked up at him from under my eyebrows and told him "Get the fuck outta here, you nasty fucking wino."

He fixed his eyes on me, little blue rings smushed between big blank pupils and swollen bloodshot red, and slurred "Fuck you, fuckin' orangeface." Then he swayed around like Stevie Wonder and reached down and grabbed my pack. I jumped up, blinking back the head rush, then lunged back at him, gripping one of the straps. He wobbled and I was sure I could just pull him off his feet, kick him away and be done with it, but then he broke his bottle on the wall and shoved it in my face. He waved it right beneath my nose, close enough to clink against the metal of my septum pierce and make me jump backward.

The shit is, when that happens, no matter who's around, you're on your own. Everyone knows everyone and the last thing you want is a beef that's not even yours. Yuppies just give the guy their wallet, cut their losses, call it even. But that shit was my sleeping roll, two pairs of underwear, socks and a knife. I couldn't call an 800 number to get it back. And getting my face slashed up by some infected wino was not on my to-do list either, but Germ wasn't much of a watchdog, and Squid was pretending to sleep on the asphalt behind me, Rusty curled up next to him like some kind of fag.

Then Critter stood up with his chain. He had to be a full foot taller than Drunk, even if he was skinny enough to disappear when you saw him from the side. The chain was tucked in Critter's knuckles and the lock at the end of it swayed more than Mr. Drunkfuck trying to get his balance, backing up and stumbling. Drunkfuck dropped my pack beside me; then he turned and ran.

Critter yelled out at his saggy denim ass: "Hey, man, aren't you gonna buy us breakfast?" Squid and Rusty just looked up at Critter like they wished they thought of it.

After that Critter and me were brothers. I don't mean that in the hippie way, like the lice-infested dreadlocked fucks hitching their way to the Rainbow Gathering who say "Hey, brother," all soft and smooth like you're long-lost family, when really they just want to know if you've got weed. I mean it in the for-real way, the way that's not the kind of shit you talk about, the way that you just do.

Pretty quick the days start blurring together. It's weird how that happens here and I think it's the weather, seventy-five degrees each day and sunny like someone set the thermostat for the city and it just runs, like a machine. Back in Utah it was desert: hot enough to cook you in the day and cold at night, wind blowing sand into your face till the sun came up, and there were seasons. Something at least to help you count the days. Not here. The weather in L.A. is like a cradle, the changes in it just enough to rock you back and forth and keep you sleeping.

I haven't gotten hungry since I got to Hollywood, mostly 'cause of Eeyore. It's a good thing her pockets are so deep; otherwise I'd get pissed off at the way she hangs around and tells us stories we all know are lies to make us think that she's a hardass, which we don't. But she's the money. It's amazing how that shit'll give you patience.

Eeyore pays for all kinds of crap: cigarettes, Del Taco, hot dogs, and people always give her change on the street because she looks so young they're scared for her. Everyone is. Bianca the trannie loved to say that just the smell of us alone could scar that child for life. Then Bianca disappeared to jail or wherever. But she must've told her little gum-snapping posse of whores to keep an eye on Eeyore between tricks, because they do. Plus the soccer moms pull up beside the sidewalk in their SUVs, call Eeyore over to their passenger windows, away from us big scary guys. They all want to find out what happened to her mom and dad, give her a ride someplace, adopt her ass, but she won't go over to the cars; Critter says the cops'll think she's tricking.

Eeyore doesn't need soccer moms or trannies, though; she's got Critter looking out for her. Some days I half expect him to help her with her homework. I could mind it but I don't, not at first at least: Critter lets her sit there, but he talks to me. When I'm around, Eeyore chills out on the bullshit braggy stories, gives us cash and sits there quiet. If she gets bored she goes over to Rusty and Squid and pets Germ. Works for me. As long as she's seen and not heard.

The old-school pimps stroll by each day at three, tricked out in James Brown hair and shiny shoes, all orange and snakeskin. The day they spot Eeyore they suddenly get interested; they slow down when they pass us, putting manners on and calling her "young lady." Eeyore just looks up at them with saucer eyes that would've got her thrown in the back of someone's Town Car if us guys weren't there. Rusty gets all squirmy like he's scared of them; Squid pulls Germ closer and looks the other way.

But Critter stares the pimps down like they're not forty years tougher than his pretty white ass. He gets right in front of Eeyore and covers her up with his shoelace-skinny shadow, shading her eyes so she won't see what they want from her. His face is brave, like nothing matters except keeping Eeyore in the dark behind him. The pimps look Critter up and down and walk on by, figuring she's spoken for. Once they're gone Critter puts his arm around Eeyore and says "Let's go get a Coke," knowing she'll pay.

The whole thing makes me realize how different it is if you're a girl.

In L.A. everyone's always locked up in their little air-conditioned metal boxes; nobody's ever on the sidewalk for more than twenty seconds except us and trannies and the drunks. We hardly ever see civilians unless we're spanging, and when we do they never look at us. I guess you get used to only seeing the people who look like you. All of this to say: unless we want some ancient junkie hooker, there's no opportunity for girls.

But a week after the pimps, this whole load of high school chicks pulls up to 7-Eleven in their yellow Hummer. These girls are insane, with shampoo you can smell, low-cut show-the-thong jeans, the whole shit. Half of them is silicone that Daddy bought—they'll melt when the shit goes down and the city burns up—but it's not like I mind, in the meantime.

When they first pull into the parking lot they're trying to pretend we're not there, like the spot of sidewalk where we're sitting is a place their eyes won't go. Everybody does it; you can see it through the windshield. But then the one with the dyed-blond hair elbows the one with the dyed-red hair and now they're all looking at Critter and you can tell they're just creaming in their pants about how cute he is, staring at him. He's skinny as fuck but he's tall, taller than me even, and he's got one of those faces with the cheekbones and the jawline, all sharp angles and symmetry, stupid puppy-dog eyes. They're still looking sideways around me like I'm an ugly building, but they're ready to take Critter back to Daddy's mansion. They probably think they can save him from his sordid life of crime. Girl shit.

The way I see it Critter's got an opportunity, but Eeyore's stuck to his side. She's curled into him like he's some pillow, smoking her cigarette down to the filter; she looks up at him when she thinks he can't see, trying to tell if he's gonna cut her loose. Her face is all open, like she needs something from him so bad she doesn't have anything left to hide it with. It kind of makes me sick to my stomach, how much of her shows on her face. Like she's asking to get hit. But Critter just stays there, doesn't look down at her but doesn't look away either, his arm around her shoulders all buddy-buddy, solid, and the girls wash up onto the sidewalk like a wave, hang there a second like they're waiting for someone to stop them, and nobody does so they push through the door and keep going. The door shuts slow on its hinge, muffling their too-loud girl laughs till you can't hear them anymore, and the whole time Critter's still got his arm around Eeyore, just staying there, and I think to myself this little kid has no idea how lucky she is.

Of course she has to push it, though. After the pimps and then the Hummer girls, Eeyore gets the idea that she's Critter's special something, and starts being heard as well as seen. She shoves her way into any conversation Critter's having, and if me and him go off, she somehow manages to always find us. Like some kind of psychic shit, how she appears at Benito's, Winchell's, Koo Koo Roo exactly fifteen minutes after we do. She's like a tick you can't pull out without the head staying stuck in your skin.

She starts showing up not just with money, but with food: Fruit Roll-Ups, Doritos, whole bags of McDonald's. Which is cool with me. The way I see it, eating her stuff is just another way of Dumpstering, living off the extra from whatever family she goes and gets her shit from. Redistributing the wealth. Critter mostly won't take the stuff she brings, though. He'll put the greasy white paper bags down on the sidewalk, nod for us to dig in, keep his hands clean. Eeyore always looks a little sad; she wants him to eat it all himself, like she cooked it for him. But she never says anything.

One time she's gone all afternoon, and comes back with her backpack stuffed like she went grocery shopping. Cheetos and salad and shit that must've been cooked in a kitchen; leftovers crammed into Tupperware, meat wrapped in tinfoil. She strolls right up into the middle of Critter and me and starts unpacking on the sidewalk. Germ smells it from five feet away and comes sniffing, ignoring Squid and Rusty when they call him. I snatch the roast beef before he drools on it, dig in and we keep talking about what we're talking about, which at the moment is girls we'd like to fuck; since no one's exactly getting any out here, it's not a conversation you want to be distracted from.

Eeyore's got some bullshit story about how she stole the food, and she's dead set on telling it to Critter. She butts in after Lindsay Lohan and then again after Carmen Electra with some invented adventure of how she almost got chased. Critter keeps saying "Mm-hm" and nodding at her, but I can tell he just wants her to go away. Finally I yell over to Squid to take her off our hands, and then I tell her to get lost. She turns to Critter like she wants him to tell her different, but Squid calls her over and she gets out of our hair. Once she walks off Critter asks me why I did that, but I know he's glad I did.

The day after that it starts raining. That only happens once or twice a year in L.A. but when it does, it comes down hard, like someone dumped it from a bucket. It floods the gutters and drowns out the fast-food breeze so you can't smell the rancid French-fry grease and the air's just soot and water. It starts pouring down when it's dark and the mosquitos get fierce; they come out like zombies awakened by the rain and keep you from sleeping the rest of the night.

You don't get downpours in Utah, almost never. It'll go years without rain and the dust gets in your teeth, dries you out till you can hardly swallow, and the dry mixes with hot mixes with whatever bruise you've got that day. But when it finally comes down it's all at once. Rain's about the only thing that happens out of nowhere in the desert; everything else you see coming for miles.

One time a storm hit when I was walking back from school; the first rain I ever saw. I showed up at home with my Teenage Mutant Ninja Turtles T-shirt wet and my stupid little mullet all stuck to my ten-year-old face. I was cold as shit but grinning 'cause it was like running through the sprinkler; I watched the dust on my knees and elbows turn to dark brown streaks and then wash all the way off, clean without a shower, and it was magic in a weird kind of way the way the sky just opened up and I was under it. I think what I did was track mud in the house and that's why I got hit that time. Or because my clothes were soaking. Every time my dad got the belt out after that I made sure I was good and dry; it stings like shit when your skin's wet.

Now it's raining for real and we're all trying to huddle under the little strip of awning over 7-Eleven. There's not many places you can go in a thunderstorm here; the city's more braced for earthquakes than rain, so we're stuck till it dries up. We stink like wet dirty jeans and dog, all crammed together, shivering.

Eeyore must've woken up at four a.m. to go for breakfast because practically as soon as it's light she shows up with coffee and oatmeal cookies in a plastic bag. She hands her extra dry hoodie to Critter. Everything is gray and blue and flooded, like the sky is washing out the city, and we just stand there watching it.

Eeyore's huddled in with Critter, keeping warm, I guess. She won't look at me. The rain must make her feel romantic or maybe just entitled from bringing the cookies, 'cause when Critter looks down she turns her face up at him and kisses him right on the mouth. Tongue and all.

The rest of us stare at the two of them like what the fuck: this shit never happened before. Rusty laughs and Squid looks sort of worried. Germ just pants and keeps on stinking like wet dog. Critter pulls away, stands there for a minute with his arms around Eeyore and his head cocked at her, squinting like she just turned into a green space alien. She opens up those big asking-to-get-hit eyes at him like some kind of puppy. He keeps on watching her, waiting for her to say something, but she just blinks up at him and kind of smiles, just a kid, not an alien, and after a second Critter stops squinting.

He shakes her little body off him like a bug, then shuffles sideways toward the three of us, leaving Eeyore just past the edge of the awning in the rain. She gets this look on her face like someone took her teddy bear away; her hair's glued to her head as drops drip down her neck into her hoodie and she shivers.

It looks like she's about to cry but then she glazes it over fast, tells Critter "Fuck off," and heads right for me with this look in her eye like she's gonna kick somebody's ass. I see her little flared nostrils and think, What the fuck, but she just comes up and puts her arms around my waist. She presses up on me different from the way she did with Critter, kind of from the front, and I can feel her tits on my stomach through her hoodie. She only comes up to my chin so she doesn't notice when I look over her head at Critter. He's smoking a cigarette she'd given him and looking west, away from us. I can't see his eyes.

Eeyore reaches up, grabs my chin and pulls my face around to her. She gives me that weird I'm-gonna-kick-your-ass look again and lowers her eyelids. I think she's trying to look hot but she winds up just looking kind of tired.

Critter's still looking away so I figure he's got no objection, and when Eeyore cranes her face up to kiss me I let her. She's so short I have to slouch way over and it hurts my neck, like sitting in the front row at the movies except the opposite; but she's pretty good for such a kid, enough to make me wonder where she learned it. And it's not the kind of shit you want to talk about, but the last time I had a girl around was Reno, which was going on a year ago, so her lips feel pretty okay. "Come on, let's go out in the rain," Eeyore says and looks at me all sleepy-eyed again. I check back with Critter one more time, but he just exhales toward West Hollywood and flicks his ash toward me.

The rush-hour yuppies sipping their Starbucks stare out at me and Eeyore from their warm SUVs like we're the TV in their miniature hotel rooms. We're a big show to them: they can't possibly imagine being unwarm and undry and not inside a cozy compartment, headed to a cubicle, headed to a little box of home. We run toward the alley, water gluing our shirts to our skin; they crane their necks at us like we're an accident they're passing by.

Eeyore pulls me behind a Dumpster and right away goes for my jeans. The rain turns trash into spitballs around us, food and paper gone soft on the asphalt, rattling off the plastic piled on top of the Dumpster. Somebody once told me it'll take three million years for Coke bottles to break down, a thousand for tin cans. All that useless shit that hangs around forever, and people just make more and more and more of it. Someday it's gonna shove us all aside. Already if you don't have a safe little house tucked away from the landfills you can see the garbage start to pile up. I look around at it while Eeyore gets down in front of me. For a second I think her knees must be hurting, gravel digging through her wet jeans, but then I forget.

When I'm done she looks up at me like she's waiting for a grade or gold star, this half-smile, half-question on her face. I hate it when girls do that shit. Everything's fine and then they have to push it, try to get some kind of answer or discussion or big moony moment. I'm not about to ruin it for myself by letting her get inside my head, so I just look at her like "What?" and zip up. She stays down on the pavement, looking up at me like I owe her an answer, getting rained on. Finally I grab her skinny elbow and pull her to her feet. She doesn't get up right away so I have to yank hard. "Come on," I say, and we head back to where it's dry.

"Fuck you, Scabius," she says under her breath like a little kid swearing at their dad, the loud of wanting him to hear it drowned out by the quiet of needing not to piss him off and get your ass kicked. She doesn't think I can hear her, but I do.

When we get back to 7-Eleven Critter's gone. I was hoping him and me could go up on Hollywood and spange for a falafel, bum some smokes. I've got this weird dirtyish feeling, like I want to wash my hands and can't as long as Eeyore's there to keep them sticky. Taking off with Critter'd clean me off.

But he's not around. When I ask Squid and Rusty what happened to him they just shrug like a couple of stoners. Squid shoots me a fucked-up look. I stare at them a minute like they must know something, but they won't talk to me. I don't know why. Finally Rusty looks up from petting Germ and tells me Critter walked off west, in the rain. Maybe he wanted Koo Koo Roo.

Eeyore's standing there with a Tootsie Pop in her mouth, her chest all puffed out like she's a guy. She followed me back but now she's looking past me. I watch her strut around, pretending brave and looking stupid, trying to protect herself from me but not knowing how to do it right, and all of a sudden I can see what she is.

It's like when you wake up sudden from a dream, blink once and the whole world around you changes. Just like that, I can see her: the whole time she's been out here, she was only faking that she's one of us.

I knew where that fucking food came from. I knew she had a house, I knew the fact of it. But I never really *thought* about it; all I cared about was getting fed. Now I realize what it means. She's one of them. She's never had her teeth knocked out, her cheek split open; nobody twisted her arm till her wrist broke, burned her skin with a cigarette down to the filter. She's never had to survive. All of a sudden I can see the mom and dad at home, waiting for her with safe wide arms to take her back whenever she slouches through their big front door. Her clothes are soaked like mine, the knees of her jeans all dirty, but she can go home, throw them in the dryer, and they'll come out soft and warm. Mine are wet till they dry stiff and itchy on my back.

The feeling of it pulls me two different ways inside, like my guts are getting yanked in opposite directions. One direction hates her for all the shit she has that the rest of us don't, using us for her street-kid fantasy when she could ditch us for some soft warm bed whenever, knowing that she will. People are loyal when they have to be, when they're the same as each other and there's no escape. When there's a hatch, they'll always take it.

But the other direction is this feeling I don't know the name of. It's got something to do with knowing she's got that soft warm bed because she's still a kid—and that Critter and me and Rusty and Squid could squash that in two seconds if we wanted to. And that maybe I just did squash a part of it back there in that alley. There's something about her that's still the way it's supposed to be, some little-kid part that could still get what it needs. And it's got about another month before it's gone. It makes me feel dirty and old and like my muscles are too strong, and I want to get her wide-open face away before she makes me hate myself more.

I go around behind, grab her waist and pull her backward, around the corner of the building. Squid looks like he's about to try and talk, but I look at him hard and he shuts his mouth before anything comes out. Eeyore gets all riled up and kicks her heels and goes "Fuck you, I'm not coming with you, Scabius," but I'm stronger, and after a second of wiggling like a freaked-out rabbit she gives up and lets me hold on to her wrist. I bring her between a Dumpster and a big red truck, to a patch of sidewalk that's still dry, and I tell her, Go home. I tell her, "We all know you have a mommy and a daddy and a house, we know you rub your T-shirts in the dirt to make them crusty, patch your jeans where they're not ripped."

Her eyes flash but I keep going, push her hard enough to shove her backward. "You're not like us; nobody really fuckin' likes you. We just eat your food. Critter too: he told me. He wishes you'd quit bugging us. Why do you think he left?"

She tries to answer but I cut her off. "Look, we know

you'll take off anyway when it's time for school in September, so why not do it now instead of waste those months pretending you're not one of them? Go home and watch TV."

Her eyes get all big; they fill up and spill over, but I don't care. I want to say something different to her, something like: You have something we all wish we did; stay away from us or we'll take it away; hard things are stronger than soft, and sooner or later your smooth skin will get cut through and you'll never not have scars again. But I don't know how to say that. So I just say "Go."

And she's gone.

That night the sky dries out and by morning the pavement dries out too. Critter's not back, though. I try heading west to look for him but I can't handle West Hollywood, the jocko guys in wifebeaters checking out my ass but hating me for being dirty, and all the stores have signs in front of them that say "The Area in Front of This Business Is Private Property. Trespassers Will Be Prosecuted." I wonder if they arrest all the rich fucks who walk on that sidewalk, or just the people who need to be there. The parking lot by Coffee Bean & Tea Leaf even has rent-a-cops to swat away the flies like me.

When it gets dark I know I'm about to get stuck without a place to sleep so I head back east. I figure Critter'll come back to where he knows we are: like when you're five and get lost in a store, you're supposed to just wait where you started, let your mom come back to find you instead of running all around. She didn't always come back, sometimes even when the store closed and it started to get dark, but Critter'll be different.

He doesn't come back that night, though, or the next or the next. Rusty still won't open his stupid mute mouth except to Squid, and Squid keeps glaring at me, asking me where Eeyore went. I tell him I don't fucking know, but he keeps asking.

By the fifth day I'm considering heading to the highway with my thumb out, back to Reno or over to Albuquerque, maybe San Diego. It must be just laziness that keeps me from getting on the 101, either that or L.A.'s worn me down too much to deal with the freeway and the fumes and the almost getting hit. Either way, though, it's good, because Critter shows up in front of Winchell's the exact day after I decide that I can't take it anymore. Or at least it's good at first, when all I see is him getting out of some rich fuck's Escalade.

Then the other door opens.

I know Tracy is trouble the first time I see her, before I even know her name. Just for a second, and then I forget I knew it. But when I see her slam the car's back door and twitch her eyes toward Critter, I can feel this bitter bile tightness that comes up in my throat, then goes away as quick as the guy in that Escalade drives off. Critter and Tracy watch the car till it's gone; then they turn toward us at exactly the same time, like someone planned it. Critter's got this shit-eating grin and his arm around her shoulder like he's some suburban husband. She has her fists stuffed deep in her pockets, pulling her pants down so you can see her hip bones sticking out like thorns.

Tracy's a full foot shorter than Critter and just as skinny, maybe skinnier. Her hair's that dingy blond that's almost green, hanging in stick-straight strings down to the bra straps on her bony shoulders, and the neck of her T-shirt is cut out so wide you can see the tops of her tattoos. She's smaller than her clothes like a kid playing dress-up, but nothing else about her is remotely like a kid. She can't be more than sixteen, but she throws off a vibe like she's older than all of us. "Hey," she goes, and tips her chin at me. I say hey back but it's weird that she talks to me before Critter does. He doesn't even ask about Eeyore.

"Guys, this is Tracy," he goes; the way he says it I half expect him to be wearing a varsity jacket. I think he's joking and I start to laugh, thinking he'll laugh too, but he doesn't. He doesn't even look up from her, but Tracy shoots me a look like I'm her stupid kid brother.

Rusty stares at her, even more retarded and mute than usual. He stutters like he's about to talk, but then he doesn't, and he keeps glancing over at Squid. I don't know what Rusty's being so freaky about: she's just a fucking girl.

After about five million seconds of this she finally says to him "What's up, I'm Tracy," and his face turns cherry-flavored red and he mumbles something stupid and goes back to his apple fritter.

Squid's the opposite: I can tell he thinks Tracy's hot, the way he flashes his not-so-pearly whites and gets all chattery and energetic. Really she looks like a rat or a weasel, but I can see what he means; she's probably a wildcat, you can tell. She has that thing the way she looks you in the face and leans her hips forward, shows her neck.

The first night Tracy and Critter are up all night like some perverted slumber party and it doesn't get quiet till the sky gets light. I'm hoping to get a decent sleep the next night, or the one after that, but instead I lie there with my back to them, curled around my stomach while they laugh the kind of laugh that only happens when you're having sex. If we had doors they'd probably close them, but we don't. No doors, no roofs, no walls was the best thing about sleeping out here, but I never had anything get in the space around my ears and stay there like some fucking mosquito. I always could slap it away. Not now.

At first I'm thinking Tracy's a temporary condition like a cold or a hangover, but pretty soon she turns into the story of my life. The two of them are always holding hands and shit, when Tracy lets him; when she doesn't he watches her sideways to see when she'll change her mind. The times when she ignores him I try to squeeze into the space it leaves between them and crack it open, get Critter to come with me to the Dollar Chinese or anywhere. But he's glued to her face, waiting, like a guy in a cubicle watching the clock.

Soon enough she turns back to him, sudden and sharp like the bell at the end of the school day, lets him know it's time. Then they take off to shoot up, find some Dumpster to duck behind. I guess I can understand it: shit lasts a lot longer shared between two people than it does between five. And I don't really like junk anyway; it's too much work, with the needles and the cooking and the blood. Beer's cleaner: in one end, out the other. But still. When they leave I always feel relieved at first, glad to get a break from their big thick vibe that spreads out and pushes at everything around them like some kind of poison cloud. I'll inhale smog and feel like I can breathe again. But then I look both ways into the space beside me, and all of a sudden there's too much air for me to swallow by myself.

It's not like I ever have to, though; they always come back no matter what I want or don't. With Critter there, Squid splits back off into fairy land with Rusty, finally leaves me alone. So it's the three of us left over. Critter, me, and Tracy. Great.

Tracy loves Benito's so we go there for chicken tacos; me and Critter split it. It's almost like a double date, us guys up at the counter ordering through the bulletproof window, but then I remember there's only one girl, which kind of throws the whole thing off. When the food comes up Critter brings it over to Tracy and they spin around on their stools and pick at the tinfoil. Steam spurts out of the holes their fingers make and I'm surprised it doesn't burn them. My burrito isn't up yet and I stay by the window, watching the big mass of meat sizzle on the grill inside the taco stand. I wonder how long it'll take for it to turn from red to gray.

For a while I watch the slab of beef change color and imagine what if Eeyore was around. It would balance things out; me and Critter could kick around the sidewalks while she and Tracy walked behind us, doing whatever girls do when they walk behind guys. Once in a while Critter and I would turn around and holler back, and they'd say something that made us laugh and then we'd all go get a 40. I could get used to it probably, having girls around for sex and whatever. I'm starting to feel okay for the first time in about ten days, waiting for my burrito and thinking about that, but when I crunch up my brain and really try to picture it I can't imagine Eeyore in the alley with us since now she's probably wrapped up safe in bed at home by dark, and then I remember that's because she's like twelve years old.

My burrito comes up; I bring it over and sit down. It looks weird when I open up the tinfoil, too big somehow and soggy, not like the neat and perfect tacos that Critter and Tracy are almost finished with by then. I try to remember when was the last time I worried about things looking neat and perfect, and then I decide I like how my food is all big and clumsy and doesn't fit with anything. Fuck them. I pull apart the gluey tortilla, leave black fingerprints on the dough. All the colors mush together when you eat it anyway.

Tracy stands up, pulls on Critter's hoodie, and says "Let's go." My mouth is full of tortilla glue so I can't tell her to hang on. I figure Critter'll pull her back down to the orange stool, spin her around till I'm done. But he stands right up like she's some general and he's started taking orders. I spit out lettuce and sour cream on the pavement telling them to wait.

Critter puffs up his chest but Tracy points her eyes down her nose and goes "No, it's okay," like a fairy god-mother granting me a wish. I still wind up choking my food down without chewing so it gums up in my throat and I can't talk.

The next day I'm on my way back down from Hollywood with donuts, two whole bags I've Dumpstered, rushing before the grease soaks through the paper. Nobody's eaten since yesterday afternoon; knowing it makes me psyched to hand over my score, like it's a Christmas present or something. Providing for the tribe. I'm almost even happy thinking how they'll say "Thanks, man," and eat.

The four of them are standing around loose and untied, shuffling on the sidewalks; then Critter looks up and sees me coming. Instead of waving hey or running toward the food, he right away goes to Tracy and wraps his arm around her waist. Tight, without taking his eyes off me. Like someone's dad.

If she'd seen the whole thing she'd've probably kicked his ass, but she didn't, so instead she just reaches down and squeezes it instead. He laughs and sinks his teeth into her neck. When I get up to them his face is buried there, his eyes looking up at me over her like Dracula. After a second he pulls his face out of her, but he keeps his arms around her waist, watching me like I'm about to make some kind of move. All I do is put the donuts down. Critter doesn't reach for them even though I know he hasn't eaten in a day. But Tracy wriggles out of his arms and goes right for the bag, sticks her grubby skinny fingers in and starts pulling donuts out, one by one. The first one she sniffs; the second she pulls sprinkles off of, the third one which is coconut she actually takes a bite from. Then she throws them on the sidewalk like they're candy wrappers. She does it with all nine donuts; then she looks up at me and says "The guy over at Winchell's gives them to me fresh." I bet he fuckin' does. "These are gross."

I don't care that she probably has a knife in her boot, I want to break her turned-up snotty little nose. She just stares at me, eyes slitted, wasted donuts ringed around her feet, chocolate and rainbow sprinkles flaked off on the filthy sidewalk. Then she takes her worn-down heel and grinds it into an apple fritter so the white insides smush out of the tan outsides and the sugar mixes up with shit-stains and dirt. She keeps her eyes on me the whole time like some kind of cowboy.

Rusty and Squid both half laugh in that nervous way you do when there's a fight starting up that you want to stay out of. I know if she was anyone else but Tracy, Critter'd be on me to kick her ass till her teeth broke, and he'd have my back too. But she's not. She's Tracy. So he looks down at her in this almost-proud way, except he's not even really looking at her, just gluing his eyes to the back of her head so they don't have to come up and meet mine. I stare right at him for thirty seconds at least. I can't say his name. Then this weird salty knot plugs up the back of my throat, and behind my eyes gets hot and I feel wet come up in them. I look down at my feet fast, but Tracy sees. "Fuckin' pansy ass," she says. Then she laughs.

The next morning Squid asks me if I want donuts for breakfast. I almost kick his ass but he says "Chill out, I'm not Tracy, man." So I tell him fuck off and take his 40 from his bag, and he lets me, which evens things out.

After the whole donut thing I went to Benito's. Even when the cops rode by three times that afternoon, circled around and drove back, I didn't leave, in case Critter came. Even when the trannies strutted by in their skanky leopard miniskirts and purple plastic heels and told me get my smelly ass into a shower, I just sat there waiting. I thought

Critter'd know to find me there, but after I watched two slabs of beef change color and he didn't show up I wondered if he thought I ditched him.

The whole next two days he and Tracy both are gone. I start thinking that it's maybe my fault, like when you lose your mom in the store and you think you might've gone to the wrong place to find her and that's why she isn't coming back. So I just wait in the places I know he'd expect me: Benito's, Winchell's, 7-Eleven. I don't even go up to Dollar Chinese. One time I take a piss in an alley I know he's never been to and spend four hours afterward wondering if he came back and I missed him.

By the time him and Tracy show up again I'm still ready to break Tracy's teeth, but she marches up to me all friendly with her hips tilted forward, stands too close and goes "Hey, Scabius, we missed you." I'm not sure if she's fucking with me so I look over at Critter. This time he keeps his face up and smiles.

Tracy goes over to Rusty and Squid, and for a second Critter and me are alone again. I sink into it like it's a mattress. I didn't know how wound up I'd been, like when you're starving and don't know it till you smell food. Now I know we'll be back in the alleys tonight when it gets dark, the sky wrapped around us, no walls, and for once Tracy'll stay quiet enough to let us sleep, and in the morning we'll scrounge each other breakfast. Maybe pizza.

I want to ask Critter if he's mad at me but I don't know the words. So instead I ask if him and Tracy found somewhere good to sleep. Maybe the crew could use a change of scenery anyway; we're always looking for new alleys. When I ask him he takes this weird pause, picking at his sleeve, and then says "Yeah, actually, but it's not someplace we could all go to," and I say "What do you mean," and he says, too loud, "Well it's a motel, it costs money," and I forget about him maybe being mad and I say "What?"

Critter and me swore back in Reno we'd never pay for a roof. It was the first thing we ever talked about, on the sidewalk staring at the Slurpee-sucking tourists who worked all day to box themselves up in walls. Critter knew it was fucked just like I did and wanted something truer, something free; that's how I knew I knew him, why he lent me five bucks and brought me here to Hollywood.

When you think someone's mind matches yours, when they tell you it does and you see that it's true, and then they go and do the opposite, there's gotta be a reason. Some force that pushes them to make them move the other way. I don't have to think too hard to know what—or who—that force is here. You could call it whipped, I guess, or sellout, but it's really worse. Tracy makes him suck up all the shit they say you're supposed to live by: four walls and bedrooms and boyfriends and girlfriends. Paying money to tuck yourself into their wasteful scared world and pretend you're so safe you don't have to try and survive. Playing house in someone else's soft warm bed with clean-bleached sheets and covers thick enough for you to hide in. She makes him want all of that and believe that he can have it too.

And the believing is the most fucked-up part of it all, because you can't have that kind of shelter; not him, not anyone; there's no place that's safe, it's all a fuckin' illusion, and believing in it eats your life away till there's nothing left but hollow walls and a hard ceiling.

I look at Critter and try to think of how to explain it to him, remind him, set him free.

The problem is he's a lost cause. I've known it since he stepped out of that Escalade with the shit-eating grin and said "Guys, this is Tracy." He's too fuckin' stoned on her to think straight, and he won't sober up. He doesn't want to. Just to test it out I ask him where they went. He stutters for a second, but then he puffs up again and says "The Vagabond Inn, you know, over on Vine," like he's bragging about some shit he scored, so proud I know it's hopeless. If I burst his bubble now he'd just blame me for being the pin-prick. So instead I crack a smile through my gritted teeth and say, "Oh yeah? That's cool, man," and start thinking of another way.

It takes a couple days, but finally I get the idea: hit her. I've wanted to do it since that day with the donuts anyway. I wouldn't have to break any bones or hurt her even, just piss her off enough that she'd decide it wasn't worth it and she'd go away. The idea comes together all at once; I guess that's what they call a stroke of genius. Inspiration. Even when I pick it apart it all works: Tracy likes Critter, sure, but she needs him less than Eeyore did, and Eeyore left when I made her. And it's not like leaving would be some big loss for Tracy. I'm sure she did fine on her own for a long time before us. So I figure it won't take that much to make her go.

I'll pull her back behind the 7-Eleven just like Eeyore; no one ever comes back there. She and I can have our little talk, I'll teach her a lesson, she'll get pissed and take off; the fog will quit clogging Critter's brain and he'll be back. It's perfect, really, the way things sometimes fit like puzzles when you see them in your head. I just have to wait till Critter leaves her side.

It doesn't take nearly as long as I think: the next night Critter has to go meet his connection at Donut Emporium, which is fifteen long blocks down. I know it takes him forty-five minutes to walk each way, plus the waiting and the deal. Plenty of time to do what I need to do and solve the problem.

Rusty and Squid are up on Hollywood, spanging or whatever; I've been the third wheel with Critter and Tracy all afternoon, waiting. I keep my eyes on the purple sky while the sun goes down and I don't even say shit when Tracy calls me Critter's bitch and laughs. It's amazing what you can sit through when you know something else is coming.

Finally the sun sinks below the low buildings and the clock inside 7-Eleven stretches its arms all the way across, 9:15, and snaps into place. Critter grabs Tracy's ass and bends down to kiss her so her back bows backward and she opens up her mouth. I stand there watching while they of course don't notice; I think to myself that I hope he likes kissing her 'cause it's the last one. I feel bad for about two seconds that he'll miss her, but then I remember it's for his own good she'll be gone.

It's different pulling Tracy back behind the Dumpsters than with Eeyore. Eeyore was little, and soft, and I knew she'd come with me no matter how much she kicked around on the way. Tracy's little too, but in this weird way she feels bigger than me, or maybe harder. That dirty too-strong feeling I'd had with Eeyore, like I was made out of rusty metal that could cut her? Well Tracy's about twenty-seven times rustier than me, and sharpened up too. I know I have to catch her quick and get her back there quicker, before she turns that rusty blade around on me.

I get her by the arm, not hard enough to make her think I'm hurting her, and say "Come on" calm enough so she'll maybe feel like it's normal, and she does. She looks up at me squinting for a second like, *What's this about*, but I just look at her like there's a reason, like drugs or whatever, and she comes with me.

When we get back there it's not like I planned, though: I just stand there. I can't hit her. Not out of the blue. It's not that I'm scared or anything, it's just too weird. Like, there we are standing in the alley, facing each other, and I can't just punch her out of nowhere, go from zero to eighty in two seconds. My muscles won't do it. I don't know how to start. Plus weirdly my throat is feeling dry and I'm all jumpy like I took some speed or something, and I don't know what to do with my hands.

But she's looking at me like I'm wasting her time, and I know I've got about ten seconds before she gives up on me and goes back to the sidewalk to keep trapping Critter in that cushy fake world, one motel room at a time, and then I'll be fucked. I have to do something.

I don't know how I got her up against the wall exactly. I just know one second my hands were heavy at my sides like they were dead and I couldn't pick them up, and after that there's this flash that sort of shoots through me and I'm on the other side of the alley, Tracy between me and the brick of the building, and I'm pressing hard enough to flatten her out, her razor ribs sticking into my stomach, her sour junkie breath in my mouth.

Her tongue is like a fish, hardly even flopping around, just laying there all meaty and thick. It makes me want to make her move it. I know she could if she wanted to.

I try with my tongue but she just keeps hers dead, so

then I use my teeth and her blood comes into my mouth all metal-tasting. That wakes her up and she slaps me, hard, one time, in the face. Her eyes look like a cat with rabies and they stop me for a second, just long enough for her to swipe at me. Her fingernails get near my eye and I pull back scared, but then I feel the pain from it spread like hot needles across my cheek and it makes me shove her by the ribs back into the wall and grab her wrist with my other hand. My muscles have that too-strong feeling surging through them harder than I've ever felt before, and I know I could let Tracy go right then, send her home like Eeyore and she probably wouldn't come back.

I know that's what I'm supposed to do, the right thing or whatever, and when I think of Eeyore's big-eyed face there's this soft little buckle that happens in my chest, squishy and so sweet it's almost rotten. But then I look at Tracy's zitty cheeks, her hickeyed neck, her skin washed out like an old paper towel, and I know the difference between her and Eeyore is that Tracy doesn't have a home to go to, and the even bigger difference is that she wants into mine. My friends, my world, my patch of street. If I let her in she'll chip away at me and Critter till there's nothing left between us but a big square of sidewalk that she'll come in and stand on. Then she'll grab him by the balls and cart him off to some pretend-safe motel and tuck him in. Away from our roofless world and everything that matters and is real.

By this time I'm hard and Tracy's limp between me and

the wall. For a second I feel her stop moving; I wonder if she passed out and I open my eyes to check. She just stares back at me glassy, like some doll or coma victim. It freaks me out for a second, how different her face is now than any time I've seen it before, all the sharp and the hard gone, just soft like sleeping. My heart clogs my throat and a little bile stings up bitter because I can't feel her breath against my neck. But then she turns her head to the side, looks down at the asphalt and breathes in, and everything's okay again.

That rabid-cat thing comes back into her eyes like she's remembering something. She rears back like she's gonna smack me another time, and I say "Yeah" to it in my head, like I'm egging on a fight. I want her to slap me again so I can hit her back. I want her to give me a reason to smash her head into the brick. I want her to do it. When I imagine it, it feels good in all my muscles, like it's what they were made for, and my teeth press together and I want to bite something till it breaks. She doesn't hit me though, the bitch. Of course. Instead she looks at me and fucking starts to cry.

Her eyes crumple up and go bloodshot: she looks like a skinny ugly baby, the kind that's wrinkled, and it's gross the way her face is just so red and raw. She keeps looking at me and it's like everything's stripped off of her, like roadkill with the skin peeled back, too goddamn fucking naked. Throw-up comes up in my mouth again, but this time more. I swallow.

"Don't," she says. "Please don't." The snot is streaking

down into her mouth, and her shoulders are shaking. I reach my hand up toward her, to smash her face or shut her mouth or something, but she flinches back into the wall and sucks her breath in loud like an asthma attack, sudden enough to stop me. I almost take a step back but I don't. "Please please please just stop, I'll do what you want just please don't touch me," she says, and she keeps looking at me, and it's like I'm paralyzed by how naked she is; I can't move.

Then I realize that she's begging, and I remember who she is, and I see that this is exactly what I wanted this whole time. Ever since she showed up on my sidewalk, Tracy's been trying to make me beg for everything that was already mine. Now it's balanced out exactly how it should be. I look up at the smoggy sky and then at her, and laugh.

She stops sniveling a second and watches my eyes, trying to figure out what I'll do next. I can see the thoughts flash across her sticky dirty face, calculating how she'll run and what she'll do and how she can make me beg again. I let her imagine it for a minute, hold on to it like something good in her hands, so she'll know exactly how I felt when she snatched my shit away from me. Then I rush her.

I slam her up against the wall. I don't care now that she didn't hit me again. She's done enough. The crying starts back up but I know it's an act: she's just trying to get me to let her go so she can go right back and steal my home away again. I'm smarter than that, though. I unzip her jeans, pull them and her underwear off her skinny hips and use my foot to get it all down to her knees while my hands pin her wrists back to the brick. Underneath my hands her skin scrapes hard against the mortar; I can feel it. It feels like her skin is mine except the bricks don't hurt me, only her. Then I'm inside and her wrists and her skin and her hurt all dissolve. They don't exist anymore; there's nothing of her that's real except for the feeling of her around me.

I don't think about Critter except I know that after this Tracy will have to leave for sure and everything can be like it was before again. Every move I make rocks things back and forth so they finally balance back to normal. The combination of that and how warm Tracy is makes me feel like I'm wrapped up in blankets, somewhere in some big soft warm bed, almost safe enough to fall asleep.

critter

i fell in love with Tracy at the Santa Monica Pier.
I can't ever tell her that. I tried to once and she kicked my
ass. Just looked at me through those slitty eyes of hers and
said if I ever said that shit to her again she'd break her beer
bottle on my face. I kept my mouth shut after that.

That one night was different though, I think because
she didn't really know me and when things happen with
strangers it's different than with people you know. Or people who know *you*, really, is what it is: Tracy thinks she can
keep anyone from getting to know her, and she gets pretty
pissed when you prove her wrong. But that first night I was
just a kid she'd seen around on the sidewalks. I knew friends
of her friends in that thing that happens on the street when
all the little circles of people link up and make a chain, but
no one I knew'd had sex with her and I didn't know her
name. We both hung out in Hollywood, so it was weird that
we wound up out at the pier, weird enough that it made us
actually smile when we saw each other, start to talk. I'd been

sleeping just south of there in Venice for a week, since the rainstorm of Eeyore and Scabius: things got too crazy up on Sunset so I took off for the beach with its rainbow fuckin' flowers and old dried-out hippies who lugged their shit around in guitar cases. Vacation. After a while I couldn't deal with the drum circles, though, so I followed the bright lights north to the pier.

It's at the arcade that we see each other. Some hyper kids are playing that old-school game where you have a bunch of plastic guys all attached to a rod and you have to slam them around so they kick the ball onto the other side. Dumb. For some reason the fact that they're yelling and jumping and getting all worked up about this stupid ancient plastic-guy game is pissing me off and I'm watching them, trying to narrow down my eyes to points so they'll turn around, be scared of me and scatter. I'm full-on focused on my goal when Tracy comes up next to me. She doesn't say anything, but I know she must've been there for a minute, because when I finally feel someone standing there she's already comfortable, leaning back on her heels with her arms crossed, copying my stance. It's weird, the switch from the feeling of total one-pointed focus on smaller-than-me people who I could've made flinch, to looking down and realizing that the whole time she's been watching *me*. My center of gravity is gone. I uncross my arms and she smirks. I don't know what to do with my hands. I smile back.

"Having fun?" she asks. I right away realize what an

asshole I look like, standing there staring at a bunch of twelve-year-olds playing whatever the fuck that game is called, and a second after that I realize that not one single girl in seventeen years of my life has ever made me feel like an asshole, ever. I want to be pissed at her but she's looking up at me with her sly little eyes through her blond stringy bangs, knowing I probably have zero retort, and she's just so fucking cute I can't hate her. "Not really," I say, and it's almost the truth.

I don't let her know till later that even right away it's fun with her around. Which is especially corny coming from my mouth because "fun" has sort of lost its edge for me; I'm not the type of person who runs around the amusement park and goes "Wow!" and is amused. Usually it takes some kind of substance, and even that's just another kind of normal. But like I said, not one single girl in seventeen years has ever made me feel like an asshole before. It's kind of fun.

"Well what the fuck are you doing in here then?" she says. "Get out," and nods toward the open door, framing lights and boardwalk and past them the black of the ocean. I look at her and then the dark and say "Okay." She leads the way.

There's not much to do out there: photo booths and whack-a-mole and rides cost money and I don't have much left today. Sometimes you can just walk around with someone and not do anything, but I don't know Tracy well enough for that. When we walk by the Ferris wheel I think of hijacking the control booth so we can swing our legs way up at the top and make everyone freak out, but the guy in there is pretty burly, and getting kicked out isn't worth it. I wish I had enough change to win her a fuckin' ugly orange teddy bear. Which is weird. The whole thing is weird, how I want it to be a Date, how I suddenly have to Show Her a Good Time like some fifties jocko guy with his ponytailed blond chick out for an evening. Usually with girls it's this: hang out, fuck, talk afterward or not. It's not like I take them to the movies or something. And she's not even hot or whatever; to tell you the truth she kind of looks like a rodent the way she squints her eyes and is so superskinny. But I don't know: every time she smiles at me, even if it's just a closed-mouth halfway smirk, I feel like I earned something.

Luckily I've got enough change in my pocket to buy her cotton candy at least. It's funny seeing her eat it, pink ringing her mouth like dress-up lipstick on a kid. For a minute I see us from the outside in our grimy black and backpacks and piercings with her toting around this Barbie-pink ball of fluff, and I laugh out loud in the middle of the boardwalk. She looks up at me with her red-stained face like I'm crazy.

It's weird how fast you can spill everything to a person if you think they're listening. That's never happened to me before, the spilling part or the listening part either, but somehow I recognize them both right away. It's crazy: Tracy tells me just about nothing about herself or where she came from; I don't know if she's got brothers or sisters or what her hometown's called or anything. Normally nobody talks about that kind of stuff, I guess, but this night isn't normal and I wind up walking along the lit sidewalk, telling her every single thing that ever happened to me practically. Next to the ringtoss she grabs my hand—well, not really grabs, more like our hands brush each other and she just hooks on—and all that shit they say is supposed to happen happens, like my chest gets all tight and my throat chokes up, and it's like wanting to fuck someone but different because I keep seeing her face and thinking how right it looks.

Right about when my fingers start sweating she says "Let's go down to the beach." You can bet I'm happy about that, but it's not even what you think—I just want to be with her in the dark where it's quiet and I can pretend she's the only other person besides me. So much of the time I wish everyone would just fuckin' disappear, and the only reason why I don't *really* wish it is that then I'd be alone. But now all those fuckers could die and I wouldn't be lonely. Two birds with one stone.

You can't go down steps or anything to get to the beach so I turn around and start backtracking to the parking lot— you can walk straight onto the sand from there. But she's like "Where are you going?" and when I tell her she looks at me like I'm stupid and walks right to the edge of the pier. You can't tell how far it drops in the dark or even if it's solid below; it could be water or cesspools for all I know and I'm not about to just jump. But she looks over her shoulder at me with a face that says *What are you waiting for?* and then she's gone. I'm not gonna walk through the parking lot after that.

It's kind of a fall, to tell you the truth. When I hit the ground my ankles jam up into my knees which ram into my hips which shove my breath hard through my chest and out my mouth. But I land on my feet, so I can swallow the ache and fake it. I amble up behind her like I'm taking my time.

Halfway down toward the water there's a place where the side of the pier is hollow and you can duck in, tucked away from the waves. It's like a wet wooden cave in there, all salt water and soft logs. You'd think it'd smell like trash or something rotting but it doesn't, it smells like sea and tree trunks, and it makes me want to take off my shoes and put my feet in the sand like some hippie from Venice. Which I don't do. The light from the pier bounces off the water and into our little hideout, waves mixing with the yells from above us, and Tracy's face is bathed in the gray-yellow glow like some underground angel and all of a sudden she's beautiful. I've never seen anyone be beautiful before. It's weird.

When she asks me if I have a bag, oh my God I've never been so happy to have drugs on me in my life. Which is saying something. I can't believe I didn't think of it myself: it's perfect. I've got a needle, too, only one but she doesn't care and when she sinks it in the smooth pale skin inside her arm

I have this flash like I'm going inside her. It makes me breathe loud enough to hear for a second but by then it's already hit her, she doesn't care, I can act like an asshole as much as I want and she won't notice the rest of the night. She hands it over to me and I could just about tell you it was better watching her get off than doing it myself, but that's only almost true.

After that I kiss her. It's like water, the feeling of it, and also like sleep, the kind that comes when you've been up three days and your head finally hits a pillow and you can practically hear every single cell sigh relief. Obviously you could also say that it's like junk, the way it floods in and makes things better, but it's different. It's not just the silk-blanket numb, the Bubble-Wrap protection from everything sharp; it's something realer, more alive. She makes me naked even though I'm still in all my clothes, the cuffs of my jeans getting heavy wet cold from the sand, and her hands feel like they're erasing every lie I ever told even though they're just hooked into my belt loops. When she reaches down for the zipper I realize I hadn't even thought of that. I mean, give me another couple minutes and I'm sure I would've, but in the sugar rush of kissing her I forgot there was anywhere else to go. I'm not used to getting distracted like that: I have to admit I usually skip to the good part. But it's like *all* of her is the good part, her mouth and her teeth and her skinny ribs under my hands and our skins melting, and we're not divided into good and bad at all.

She pushes ahead faster than I would, but it's fine: the normal equipment problems junk causes are miraculously not in attendance and mostly I just care that she's close to me, I don't think about order or speed. She unbuckles and unbuttons, lets my clothes fall to the soaking ground and keeps her T-shirt on; I run my hands under it like it's sixth grade except this time I know how to unhook her bra. She's so tiny underneath: my arms circle around her like our little cave surrounds us, like the ocean wraps around the whole pier and even the city, and the whole time *I'm* inside *her*. She's the only person that exists besides me. I don't have to pretend.

The next morning I wake up sandy, dried-up ocean caked in my eyelashes. The beach is full of burned-out coals and green glass bottles; the pier looks empty with the Ferris wheel paused and the lights dimmed down, like a play set or a skeleton. Tracy's still asleep next to me. It's the first time I get a good look at her, really, without her watching. She must've lost her T-shirt eventually, because she's curled up in her bra and I can see her tattoos. India ink, mostly, and crappy. She looks different in the light, paler, her back scratched up and full of zits. Her body is all white and scabby red and bones, but I know I must love her because instead of being grossed out I just think she looks like some kick-ass alley cat.

I don't want to wake her up because I know when I do

it'll be the weird thing of what's going to happen next. Usually that thing only lasts a few minutes because I say I need some coffee and take off. But I have a feeling Tracy's more like me than I am: probably she'll be the one needing coffee, and I kind of want to drag this out forever. If I have to let her sleep the whole time it's okay as long as we both can still stay here.

What's crazy is when she wakes up she sticks around. I keep waiting for her to do all the shit that I do: throw her eyes over my shoulder like she's looking for something, stop talking, start making excuses. Or else play the girl part and get all clingy, although I kind of know that isn't gonna happen. But she doesn't do any of it. She just pulls on her hoodie, yanks my stocking cap off and wipes her eyes with it, and says "Come on, let's get a donut."

We wind up hitching all the way back to the Winchell's on Hollywood. I can't believe the two of us get a ride looking the way we do but we do, and end up winding down Sunset, taking the curves too fast in the back of some rich guy's Escalade who probably thinks we'll go home with him but is too sweaty and shy to ask. All through Bel-Air and Beverly Hills I think about holding Tracy's hand and don't do it. But she comes back with me, all the way back to Winchell's, and winds up sticking by my side when we hit my normal sidewalks and I introduce her to my friends and then finally I let myself think, Maybe she'll stay around for a while.

I don't make predictions about people, except I can tell when someone's gonna be an asshole. What I mean is I don't expect anything from anyone, not ever, really. You can't. At some point everyone will always fuck your friends or hit you or hit you up, steal your shit when you're sleeping, suck your energy like a vampire or lie. Including me. But everything's been different so far with Tracy, so like a dumbass I let myself think maybe she'll be different that way too. To tell you the truth I guess I've got some kind of stupid hope that comes from somewhere in the same vicinity as that fifties jocko win-her-a-teddy-bear shit. I mean, I can't deny it. But I'd never tell her that.

For a while we do it everywhere. I never knew L.A. was so big. We get to know practically every underpass beneath the 101: Franklin, Gower, Sunset, Western, Santa Monica also known as historic Route 66. We duck just behind the guardrails two feet from the road and if we want to talk we have to yell above the cars. Mostly we don't want to talk, though.

It's amazing how a person can make a place feel different. I thought asphalt and concrete all looked the same till Tracy started taking me places and I started noticing things like smells and potholes and how each place we go is specific in a way I couldn't even describe to you, except to say they're all exactly themselves at exactly those moments in a way that is secret and ours. The other thing that's crazy is that the whole thing makes me start using words like *amazing* and *secret* and *ours*. A month ago I would've heard that and called myself a corny naive little shit. I mean, it's not what you'd think, all soft-focus lenses and movie bull-shit, where the guy gets the girl or vice versa, and everyone laughs about how adorably awkward they are, and at the end you sniffle in your hanky and clutch the hand of whoever's next to you. It's not like that. It's just that we both have these edges that've always scraped up against everyone around us, but somehow with each other they line up so they fit together perfect and no one gets cut.

I've never known how to not hurt someone before, and I'm pretty sure she hasn't either. It gives us permission, I think, and beneath the overpasses, in the ditches, behind the Dumpsters in the alleys we rip into each other pretty good. She always leaves scratches on me and sometimes she shoves her hands up against my throat and keeps them there, shaking, while I kiss her. I know she'd never hurt me so I let her do it, even when her eyes go weird and she pushes me back against the Dumpster hard enough to bruise my spine on the rusty green metal, even when she yanks on my hair till it comes out in her fingers, when she bites down on my shoulder and takes out little bits of skin. All that shit makes sense to me in this weird way, like it clicks with something in my brain: it's right for her to do it. Sometimes she hits me when she comes, her hands hot against my chest and arms, and I feel like a kid, like home, this weird time warp into something familiar and black and outside of my skin. Then she'll stop, finished, and I'll open my eyes, see her little naked body there, and this feeling of *myself* will rush back into me hard and fast enough to hurt.

We never get high until afterward. I wish I could tell you it's like that first night over and over, that we shoot up and every time it's some crazy aphrodisiac thing where I'm man enough to overcome the junk and give it to her good. But that's not really the deal. We tried one more time after the pier to do it like that—shoot first, fuck second—with pathetic results. I would've been totally embarrassed if it weren't for the fact that I was high and therefore didn't give a shit. She didn't either. But I learned my lesson. Every time after that I make sure we start making out before she can go rooting around in my backpack. When we're done I pull out cigarettes for us to smoke while I cook up the shit, and then we do it like falling asleep in each other's arms. Better than cuddling, I'll tell you that much. Plus it kind of sidesteps the whole thing of guy-wants-to-sleep, girl-wants-to-talk, which probably wouldn't ever happen with Tracy anyway, but whatever.

I'd be happy if this time would last forever. Even if forever was really fuckin' short and I had to die at the end of it. I mean, she even hangs out with my friends, who up till now have been the only thing I'd ever call important—although you know I'd never say that to their face. Girls usually think they're a bunch of fucks, especially since Eeyore's gone and there's no cute-factor left. Eeyore'd already split when Tracy and I got back: home to Mom and Dad, I figured. Now it's just Rusty and Scabius and Squid, all crusty guys like me who sit around and stink and swear at people on the sidewalk. But they're pretty much all I've got in Hollywood or anywhere, so it's cool that Tracy doesn't make me choose.

Everything about her is cool; that's the thing that kicks my ass. Her India-ink tattoos, stringy cigarette-blond hair, how her ribs poke my chest when she leans up against me, the way every once in a while she quits slitting her eyes and I catch them wide open, reflecting the glow of the lights all around us and I just watch her like that without telling her. Plus, of course, the following facts: she curses better than any of my friends, fucks like a goddamn rabbit, and never wants to talk but somehow understands everything I'm ever thinking like some fuckin' telepathy. She matches me.

I even start to come into money after hanging around her for a while. I guess she must make me more appealing to the masses, or at least less scary, because all of a sudden the guys up on Hollywood start taking me up on it when I mutter "candy" out of half my mouth. I'd always had enough sales to get along, but it was all to kids I sort of knew. But now we plop down on the sidewalk by the wax museum and when the junkies come by Tracy gets all excited and says "Let me do it," like we're hitching and she wants to be the one to stick out her thumb. She's cute about it, like a little kid. And people stop for her. Guys who'd never duck into an alley alone with me are all about stopping when Tracy cocks her head sideways and makes the offer. She trails us around the block, watches the deals go down like I'm some rock star and she's my manager or something, making sure nobody stiffs us. It's like her job.

Sometimes the guys we sell to think they'll get something else out of it too. I can tell, the way they hang around after, flick their eyes back and forth between me and Tracy like they're watching Ping-Pong. Sometimes they'll stay on her too long and I'll hock a big one on the sidewalk, making sure they remember I'm there. Then they look back at me and straighten out their sleeves, pretend they're thinking about something else besides fucking my girlfriend. I don't know what they think: that I'll just say "Here, you can have her," or that I'm pimping her or what. Whatever it is, it's bullshit. It makes me feel sick to my stomach, actually, like here's this thing that's real and mine and they just want to blur it back into the rest of the world and make it disappear. She never says anything to them, though, and she won't look at me either. She just stands there and watches the guys like she's waiting for someone to tell her something.

Pretty soon we rack up enough money in a day to get a real bed. My boys down on Sunset don't like that too much, me leaving them out on the street while I yuppie it up in clean sheets. Cable TV and a bathtub: of course they'll wind up jealous. But I'm sure they'll understand. The cops have been circling around more than usual, leaning out their windows like they want something from us, and there's only so long you can convince them they've got nothing to arrest you for. And besides, Tracy and I could use a little privacy.

The first time, we try to stay in this motel called the Vagabond Inn over on Vine. I like the name. Little pink stucco place with aqua trim and a Coke machine by the pool. I've got a whole fantasy going about it, the lock on the door and the box spring and the shower, me and Tracy in the big bed pointed toward the TV; I've been eyeing it since we started making money. They have an ice machine there, too. I recognize ice machines from a trip I took back when I was a kid; I don't know where the trip was to or what we did, but I remember the orange-and-brown plaid carpets in the hall, how I walked on them to get a plastic pail full for my mom so she could ice her face. That's all I remember. Anyway, my plan is to bring a bucket back to our room at the Vagabond Inn and run the ice all over Tracy's body so it'll melt into little rivers in the dirt on her skin, and she'll shiver, clean in the spots where I touch her.

Unfortunately, the guy who runs the place is a fucking shit. He looks right at my grimy shirt and Tracy's tattoos and says "Sorry, you can't check in without a credit card." He doesn't even ask if we have one. Stupid fuck. I've never wanted a credit card in my life, but right now I want a Platinum Visa so bad, just so I can rub it in his fucking face. What I could do without the Visa is punch him, but there's bulletproof glass between us, and a counter where you slide the money back and forth. I guess that's why they put the glass there, to keep the people who own shit safe from people like me. Stupid Fuck says "Just below Santa Monica there's a hostel, they take cash." Tracy tugs at my sleeve and says "Come on." On the way out I spit on the glass.

So the hostel is our lap of luxury the nights we can afford it. Guys' rooms and girls' rooms are separate with twelve bunks in each one and bars on the windows; it's not exactly ice machines and free HBO. Not gonna brag to my boys down on Sunset about bringing her *here*. But the halfway-house dropouts doze off early, and once they're snoring Tracy and I sneak into each other's rooms, stay up all night and use the chlorine-smelling showers. Her hair smells better dirty.

It's in the hall outside the girls' room that we fight the first time. Actually it started on the street, but our beds are paid for so we wind up taking it inside. Here are the facts: we've been selling enough shit to run out, my old connection's fucked, the cops are everywhere, and Tracy finally found a guy she says can get us more. I was supposed to be at Donut Emporium at ten with the money; I was fifteen minutes late. The guy left, I spent the next two hours circling the block trying to find him. By the time I gave up and got back to Benito's it was after midnight. Tracy wasn't there.

Scabius spun on an orange stool, drinking a 40 alone in

the fluorescent glow, face flushed and clothes mussed like he'd been in a fight. He gave me this weird creepy grin but said he had no idea where she was.

Now I find her four blocks down in front of the hostel, rocking herself on the curb, her eyes bloodshot and empty. I've never seen her eyes like that. She doesn't notice me, staring into some tunnel only she can see. I'm half a foot away by the time she startles out of it, and then she freaks on me like a cat who's eaten someone's speed. "Where the *fuck* were you?" she screams, loud enough to make the actress-type parking her Miata ten feet away turn around and look. "You were supposed to be back two *goddamn hours* ago!" She never cared how long I've been gone before.

The empty in her eyes fills up; now they're wild, shining like she might cry just from being so mad. I notice blood on the backs of her hands, like they got scraped on brick or sidewalk. Her clothes are stretched out and ripped, and she's jumpy: digging into her arms, leaving bright pink trails and little bloody moons. It's almost like she's more than angry, crossed over into some other kind of territory hotter and sharper than anything I've seen.

I don't even know why she's so weird and mad except it's been two days and she must be needing junk. It seems like more than that, but something stops me from asking. I just try to calm her down. I pull Tracy in off the street so Miata lady will stop staring. When I grab her arm she slits her eyes at me, hissing: "Don't you ever fucking touch me again." She means it, I guess: when I ignore it and yank her inside, she reaches up with her free arm and rips at my hair, squealing. I push her off me, but I think it makes her mad how easy it is for me to get out of her grip, because she starts fighting like a girl, all sharp teeth and fingernails and nasty words. She says all this shit to me: I never fucking show up when I'm supposed to, if I'm not gonna come through why the hell is she fucking me, I'm not worth the work it takes to fake it. I think she's trying to get me to hit her, but I just stand there while she freaks out snarling like a pissed off mean little dog.

I don't know. Usually I want to kick people's asses when they fuck with me. And it's not that I love Tracy so much I can't hit her or some shit like that. I don't think love has anything to do with it. Just for some reason I can't click into the place where she is. It's like in cartoons when the bad guy backs you up against the wall and at the very last moment you just vanish and reappear behind him, turn yourself to nothing, never real enough for him to catch.

After that I know I can always be invisible if I need to. It makes me hate her a little, that I can't count on her to catch me, that she'd let me slip out of her grasp like that. I'd never do that to her.

I don't believe in prophecy or fate but you have to admit it's pretty fucking weird that me and Tracy have our first fight the very same night Laura rolls into the city and checks into the girls' room. I can look back and feel that girl through the wall, and it comes down on me like a too-hot blanket, the doom of it, how that night Tracy started to leave. It's weird how things can seem just like life when they're happening but when you look back later you see it was all part of some inevitable plan that's a thousand times your size.

I should've taken the cops as a sign. Cops are a bad omen, always. They keep trolling around more and more till suddenly it's twice a day, and finally they get out of their cars and come up to Scabius and me, hard, hands on their belts, and ask us what we did with Eeyore. I guess she didn't go home to Mommy and Daddy after all. I stay cool, despite the copious amounts of shit in both my pockets. Officer Asshole swivels his bulging stubbly face toward us; from the corner of my eye I can see Scabius sharpen up. I start talking fast so Scabius can't butt in and screw it up: lots of "Officer" and "Sir." I tell the cops that Yes we know Eeyore and to look in Venice, so they'll stay away from us. They do. At least for now.

There are too many bad signs around all of a sudden: the cops, the fight, Tracy's weird mad bloodshot eyes. But I'm still clueless, too wrapped up in my little lovesick world to let myself believe that something's wrong.

Because at first it's just like: okay, Tracy has a friend. That's cool. It happens. Just another kid come to L.A. from the desert for refuge. But Laura isn't one of us; she's an outsider. And outsiders will fuck with you. You can tell: she's not hard enough at the edges to be really running from anything, and her yellow T-shirt's spanking clean, brown hair pulled back in a ponytail that looks like it's been brushed ten times just today. She's even got earrings, not safety pins or steel rings but real ones, little hoops made out of gold. And she latches on to Tracy like a baby sister or a crushed-out kid.

But Tracy likes her, so I make nice. I'm all gentlemanly and shit, letting her and Laura have their little pow-wows or whatever. I keep my mouth shut when Tracy stops hanging out with the guys, pulling me out of the pack, away from them, without even saying hello. She tells me to keep Scabius the fuck away from her, always, every second, and I do. I don't even make a fuss when Tracy takes off with Laura for a while. I know she'll always come back and find me at Benito's, pull me back into the alley where it's too dark for little-girl Laura to see, and Tracy and me will be back alone in the asphalt and dirt and the steel of the Dumpsters. We stay on schedule, meeting up near noon and five and then again at night; one time out of three we fuck first and the others I just lean up against her, close my eyes. I count on it like I'd count on a watch if I wore one and I know she won't slow down on me or stop.

The problem is it all starts shrinking. Before, Tracy and I would crisscross all of Hollywood, underpass to underpass, block to block. Every place belonged to us in the way that places do when you find them together, and L.A. had more ground than we could ever cover so the world called Ours stretched out for miles. But now I'll say *Come on, let's go out by the 5*, and she'll be like *I'm tired, I need to be nearby, I want a taco*. She says she likes the alley by Benito's, she feels safe like it's home, and I sure as hell have never seen Tracy give two shits about feeling safe but I go along. We memorize that alley: green chipped paint on the rusted Dumpster, rats in the cracks, the brick of the buildings against our heads. And you know I could even get into it in a cozy settled-down way if the time part didn't go and start shrinking too.

But guess what, it does. Tracy shows up and pulls me back there by the hand and it isn't like before, where there was this bubble around us and we'd get so lost it was scary and cut-loose and right. Now her hands are lazy and pushy all at once—but not pushy in the good way of wanting, pushy in the way of getting it over with. When I shove her up against the wall she just lays there and her eyes go blank. She never looks at me. She doesn't shove back like she used to, and my skin stays smooth, unscratched. I miss the marks she cut into me. I feel too clean.

It's weird to think about what I'd be if Tracy'd never happened. I start thinking about that a lot after a while, once Laura starts looking like she's sticking around, once Tracy goes off and has her dyke affair or slumber party or whatever and forgets everything that's important and real.

See, I'm still using shit words like *important* and *real*. I swear to God that girl turned me into a pussy.

At first it weirds me out, because everything still seems kind of normal. You know, she has her friend, she comes back to me, we eat tacos, we fuck, we shoot up. But there must be some part of me that knows it's different already, because I start imagining all the time: what if Tracy was gone. I'll be sitting with Scabius and Rusty and Squid and just space out, trying to remember what it was like before Tracy, and they'll be like "Man what is *wrong* with you" just as I'm realizing I can't remember it without her. I just can't. It just seems like a big empty pit, like a blackout where afterward everyone tells you you said shit and did shit, but no matter how many details they give you none of it feels real.

I start counting the time she's gone. When the two of them take off I shuffle my feet outside Benito's, trying to front like I don't have an eye on all four directions in case she turns a corner, comes back into frame. I camp out by the hostel door, squat on the sidewalk with the trannie whores. When they try to pick me up I tell them to fuck off. They say "What, you waiting for your girlfriend or something?" and I just stare off at the hills because there was no way I'm gonna tell them the truth, which is yes.

Then I start doing things to try and hold on to her. Shit like asking where she's going and when she'll be back, and then showing up at McDonald's or Tang's Donut just to let her know I'm checking. Like listening to the words she uses, slipping them into my sentences so she'll think I know her mind. Copycatting, watching, trying to slide into her shadow. Pussy shit, too: I even stick up for her stupid friend. The one time in forever that the two of them come around my crew, run into us by accident at Benito's, Scabius pipes up. He calls Laura "Country Girl," tells her to give him a blowjob or get out. He's kidding or whatever, and it's ridiculous how girl Laura is about it, all serious and lame, but she just won't budge from her little-baby stance. Finally Tracy freaks out on Scabius, gets all weird and spits on him and tells him to fuck off. I back her up. I know I'll get shit for it later, but whatever. All I can do right then is watch what Tracy does and try to copy it so she'll be happy.

But I can't make her be; she keeps running back to Laura who I'm sure keeps telling her some shit about some kind of category I'm part of, some category that really means: *not them*. Not their little perfect frilly fuckin' world. It's like they have some kind of secret, even though I know there's nothing Tracy could tell Laura that's as real as the things she says to me without talking. I may not know the facts of Tracy, but that's only because nobody does. I know everything else.

I know everything and I can see straight through her, and the night of the day of the Scabius blowjob incident, right before the sun sets, Tracy comes over to see me when

Laura's up on Hollywood spare-changing for their tampon fund or whatever. I see right through the surface of her eyes like it was plastic wrap. I know she wants junk and that's why she came back.

She's all like "Sorry about before, I know I was sort of a bitch," and even though *I'm* the one they think is a bitch, I'm like "Yeah, well, whatever." I can't look at her: I know Tracy is constitutionally incapable of saying sorry and meaning it, but at the same time that "Sorry" is the thing I want most of all, and there she is saying it.

It's weird, hearing what I need and knowing that it's just a lie, like wanting to be touched and having someone hit you. It still feels good even though you bleed. It's the best you can do. And sometimes it's enough: sometimes you settle, and you start to look forward to getting hit because at least someone's hand is on your face, at least there's something else touching you besides cold naked air, at least something makes the blood rise, and the tingling in your skin keeps you warm for a while. But then there are times when it turns to an insult, a mean joke that reaches into your ribs where you keep the buried shit, the shit you need, the shit you never say, and pulls it out and holds it up in front of you and everyone like dirty underwear. And everyone laughs but you can't, and you can't cry either, and you also can't stand there but they won't let you run and the hole in your ribs lets the air in and the bubble of it swells and swells inside you till you pop.

I hit her. I hit her hard and her cheekbone pokes into my knuckles like a rock or a knife, sharp, and I know if I'd been one step closer, if she'd been one second less ready, I'd have shattered it. Her face would've caved like giving in to me, like surrender, the sharp of her would've gone soft and I would've won.

But she doesn't, I don't, instead her cheekbone rams into my knuckles bruising the hell out of my hand, and it's just another fucking blow to me, just another way she kicks my ass even though there she is bleeding through her fingers dripping brown onto the sidewalk and she looks up at me with her fuckin' stupid-ass weepy eyes, faking that I hurt her feelings, and I know she'll cry to Laura who'll stand in solidarity against me as the big mean nasty guy. Bitch. I can't stop getting my ass kicked by Tracy even when I throw the punch.

After that, I keep going to the spot by the Dumpster to look at her blood on the sidewalk. There are five drops of it, dirt-brown like liquid rust on the grit of the asphalt, perfect circles. Weirdly it's beautiful, the residue of her, beautiful like the gray-green glow off the Santa Monica Pier, like the alley-cat scratches on her bony shoulders. It's beautiful because it's real, and because I made it happen, but most of all because no one knows what it is. If anybody ever even saw it they'd think it was shit or dirty gum ground in the sidewalk, but they'd never think of it as blood from someone's face. It's a secret I have with Tracy: I can see her whenever I want. If I squint hard enough I can almost see her face in it, or sometimes her cells, all the parts of her she hides from everyone. She thought she could hide them from me too, but she can't. That's the thing of it. She walks through the world so tough, her and Laura holding hands and whispering like it's fourth fucking grade and they have some world nobody else is part of, but the secret is that I can see right through the walls around that world. It doesn't matter whether Tracy thinks she's letting me look; I can see everything inside her.

Now it's the day after that night, the night she'd probably call The Night I Hit Her, and my knuckles hurt. Her face was so sharp it scratched my skin across the bones, and now they're swollen up like purple popcorn; I keep my hands in my pockets because I really don't feel like getting into it with Scabius and Rusty and Squid. They'd just be like "Fuck yeah, you showed her" and reduce it to their level, which is nothing like the real of it, the secret real of it where Tracy made me swell inside till I burst through my skin and burst hers too and now I can see inside her when I want. There's no way they'd ever comprehend that, and besides if I told them it wouldn't be a secret anymore, tucked down between me and her; they'd be able to go out by the Dumpster and see her too. And that's bullshit. So I stuff my hands down in my dirty pockets and keep quiet, and when Tracy marches up to me with her purple-as-a-sunset cheek I grab her arm and pull her down the block.

* * *

I can tell when I see her that she has big plans. She's probably gone over and over it with Laura, exactly how she'll tell me off, bring me down notch by notch by notch. She's trying to puff her skinny chest up like some bird or animal, but her ribs are tiny; I can see right through her.

"I'm fucking quitting," she says; it's the first thing out of her mouth. "I'm taking off and quitting so that I don't have to eat your fucking shit, and I don't care if it hurts and I puke till my stomach's dry, so don't even try to tell me that's what'll happen. I don't fucking care because it's better than having to fuck your sorry scabby ass. I'd rather puke up blood than ever touch you again, so fuck off and go find some other bitch to pollute with your nasty fuckin' jizz." That's what she says. And then she turns around and walks toward Hollywood.

If I was smart I'd run after her, grab her shirt and make her stay. But I have that cartoon-invisible thing again where I vanish and reappear behind her, turn myself to nothing, and it slows me down, way down so when she walks away all I can do is stand there watching. She's walking north and the mountains are beyond her soaking in the gray-blue smog, Hollywood sign half hidden by it. It's like at the ends of movies, like she thinks that she's some cowgirl on some screen riding off into the distance alone. Pretty soon the smog will swallow her up and she'll just disappear.

laura

*b*urbank *never changes. It's one big plastic strip*
mall, run together through the base of the hills like a thread,
Jamba Juice Bed Bath and Beyond and nail salons like
whorehouses, buff and frost like blowjobs for the rich white
lonely women. On Cahuenga the road hugs the freeway and
the lanes narrow, squeezing you tight between hill and highway, birthing your car finally into wider lanes, the spit and
grime of Hollywood, and no matter who you are or where
you've been it always feels the same.

Six years ago I was here, speeding down Ventura with
my feet on the dash of a clunky red truck, and now I'm here
again inside some stranger's Accord, and years have inter-
vened giving my fingers their first faint wrinkles but it all
looks the same out the window. When we drove through
before, my mom pointed at the storefronts like they were
somehow glamorous but I never believed her: sure, they
were new and bigger than the things I'd seen, but even then
I saw the grime around the plastic.

We were here for Disneyland. We drove down 40 then 15 from Ludlow till the desert turned to endless suburbs, six hours of traffic till we got to Anaheim and found out they raised the entrance fee. She got pissed off because we couldn't afford it, and plus the motel rates were jacked up for the tourists—Motel 6 cost eighty bucks a night. So we went up to L.A. I didn't mind, not really—I was ten, already too old for Mickey, Minnie, Dumbo, and all them. The whole thing had been my mom's idea. I think she thought it was obligatory, proof of her maternal commitment and skill. I remember thinking it was kind of a crock. I knew she was more interested in L.A. than Disneyland anyway, the promise of the city, the way the letters stretched across mountains and it looked how it looked on TV.

It still looks like that up in those hills, and down at their feet it's still plastic and dirty. It's weird, the way so many things happen but the ground stays the same, how we turn inside out, molt, grow new cells while words endure: HAIR. CELEBRITY AUTO BODY. MEL'S. You could call them institutions but really it's just that here in Los Angeles signs are built to withstand earthquakes, and we are not. I remember my mom told me what a fault line was while we were here and I thought every highway traced a place where the ground could open up and spill us all into the sea. I remember thinking that would still be better than going back to the desert. At least it would change something.

But now it's been six years and I'm back here and

nothing's changed but me. I don't think places are what make you change. My mom always talks about them like when we get there something will happen, but there's always a reason we don't get let in. And when you're looking from the outside, everything is just itself, the way they've built it, not what you've built it up to be.

A few weeks ago I said fuck it. I didn't mean to, not really: it wasn't the kind of thing where I packed my bag and had it hidden in the closet, tracked my mom's routine so I knew she'd be at the grocery store, plotted the escape. You always hear of kids running away like that, leaving notes, but that's not what I did. It was more like this: one morning I got up at noon, took money from my mom's secret coffee can, walked out the front door through the orange dust and crossed the blacktop to the 58. There was a truck. I put out my thumb. I'm sixteen and a girl so he stopped. I got in.

We drove toward Hinkley, not so much where I wanted to go, but then I wasn't trying to go anywhere in particular. He looked at me like I was bait and tried to be my friend. I rolled my eyes and spat out the window. It wasn't what he thought: me some little wounded hitcher girl and him the big sexy teacher or the bad guy. It was more like the times my mom's boyfriends told me I was pretty. My skin was pasty and my hair was dull brown and my body was just medium. I knew I wasn't pretty. They all thought I rolled my eyes and shut my mouth because my daddy had hit me my boyfriend had dumped me or something, but really I'd just had about enough. "Such a shame," they'd say, and my mom would say "It is, isn't it?" It was more like that.

It is, isn't it. She had a few of those—phrases she used over and over, even if the people and places and rooms were different, even just with me. When I was little it was Disneyland she talked about over and over, and Someday; after that failed trip it was pretty much whatever the current boyfriend said. There were lots of those, boyfriends, and I got over trying to like them after I turned twelve or so. She liked them well enough for both of us.

She would've liked this guy, too, with his green truck, gritty grin, dirty hair. Around the truck stops I'd smile at him just enough so he wouldn't get bored and drop me off. Other times I watched the desert through his bug-stained window. It was flat and June already, and my arms smelled like sweat, the kind that's still faint enough to be sweet; no salt, just skin and heat.

We got to Hinkley, and he said "Here we are, end of the line. Unless you want to stay and ride around a little. . . ." My mom taught me how to say no thank you, so I hopped out at the BP, walked west like I was going somewhere and knew where it was.

The rest of it was pretty much the same. I got five rides, south and west; on the third one I figured out I was going to Los Angeles. It was past eleven and the stars stretched out wide, glinting in the empty, and they reminded me of nighttime city. I said it out loud, a mark on the big quiet blackness like a star. After that I'd tell them my destination and they all thought I was nursing some kind of dream.

None of those L.A. dreams are worth much, though. I figured that out back at ten years old when I watched my mom blink back the strip malls, drive around looking for things that sparkled till even the sky was grime, race toward Grauman's Chinese to find the hooker standing in Gene Kelly's footprints. Eventually she took me home. The city tries to feed those dreams, painting buildings pink and pasting posters everywhere, stars shining down on you bigger than your car, but the dirt gets in all the cracks like they're creases in your hands and makes your palm prints filthy, and anything you were trying to find that was shiny gets dull fast.

I guess I came here looking for a different kind of dirty than the one I knew. I'd memorized every inch of Ludlow, the neon and the highway and the dust, and the thousand or so words that people used; I'd used them up. I'd burned through every book in my tiny school library, made straight A's since seventh grade and no one noticed: not my mom, not my teachers even. Past twelve, if you were a girl, all anyone cared about was pretty. Words swarmed inside my head like bees, and everyone around me was afraid of getting stung. So I sat there silent, picking at my cuticles in English class, peeling my split ends apart at dinner. Heading out to the porch when my mom switched on the nightly parade of glossy packaged people through our tiny TV. *Shy*, people said, or *Sullen*, or *Isn't it a shame*. It is, isn't it. I had all these sentences in my brain, so many more than my mom ever used, and all anyone ever said was *Too bad, she could be so pretty*, when I knew I couldn't.

I was bored I guess is what it was, and I wish I could say something more interesting like I had a goal or dream or there was something I was chasing but there it is. My mom could do without me, I was tired of TV, I came to L.A. by accident with a couple hundred bucks and a school I.D. from Ludlow High, hoping to find someone who at least knew how to talk.

He drops me off at Hollywood and Vine, by a big billboard that says "Angelyne" and has a picture of some blow-up doll with big tits swathed in pink. Down the street there's one for Spearmint Rhino Gentlemen's Club, and the first thing I think is that's the most fucked up name for a strip bar I have ever heard. What happens with kids like me in Hollywood is they become strippers or do grainy porn on cheap videotape in some guy's basement and then get killed. I've seen enough TV movies to know that. But seeing it blown up full size above my head is another thing entirely, because some guy said about those girls: *She could be so pretty* and then painted her and stuck her up there. It's real, the fake of it and the glossed-over raw, and it makes my ribs feel dirty.

A couple blocks below that is the hostel. I asked my last ride, a puffy Honda-driving guy who worked in "the industry," which he explained to me meant movies, where I should stay. I said it so pissy and mean that there was no way he could suggest his place. He said south on Vine there was a Vagabond Inn, and below that he thought he'd driven past a hostel once. Just when I'm starting to lose hope I find it. It's eight bucks a night for a bunk bed. It's like two in the morning and there's nobody up. I climb in my bed in the girls' room I'm assigned and look out the window. You can see HOLLYW stretched across the mountains and then a building cuts it off.

That first night there the screaming wakes me up. That sounds dramatic, doesn't it, like some crime or sordid thing. Really it's just Tracy, this girl about my age with bleached-out skin to match her hair, pale yellow, yelling at her gorgeous, sketchy boyfriend before he goes back to the guys' room or the street. He keeps saying *Tracy* over and over, like her name would make her listen. But she's really upset, enough to be scary; he was late to something or other and she's determined to rip him a new one. I try not to let my eyes crack open; I don't want her to turn that flood on me, and besides, it's none of my business. But by the time he shuffles off to his side of the building I am definitely up.

Right before dawn has always been my favorite time. In Ludlow the sky is clear like glass above the gray-brown sand, the blue darker than daylight and lighter than night, the only deep, real color you ever see in the landscape around there. I used to wake up sometimes for no reason and lay in the sheets just to watch it. I could've snuck outside to see the sunrise, but it was so quiet I thought if I even rustled the bedspread I'd stir it all up. Sometimes a truck would roll through from Cleveland or Michigan or somewhere, but somehow their noise was part of the quiet too, like the tree in the forest with no one to hear. Except me, but I could keep the secret.

Here it's different. The blue is the same but the sounds are louder, not like trees in forests. Here they're starting their days already, the first wave of them, padding out to get newspapers, turn keys in ignitions, beat the traffic. Someone breaks a bottle on the sidewalk below us. When I look down later it's still there, green like grass or emeralds, glinting on the gray of the pavement.

Tracy's three beds over from me and she keeps trying to readjust her sheets like it'll make her warmer, cover her up. She humphs and rolls onto one side, wiggles herself into the covers and stays still for twenty seconds, then starts it all again. I see her mid-roll, when she flails the sheets off before swaddling herself. She's rat-faced and skinny and her hip bones poke through the thin synthetic blanket. She's been crying. Her clothes are black and she has pins and patches everywhere, spikes around her neck like a too-tough dog. I'm scared of her. I fall back asleep.

By the time I open my eyes again it's almost one. The sun is hot through the windows and I wake up sticky, filmed with gray like the haze on the mountains, blurred. All the other bunks are empty, and I'm relieved I won't have to stand in line for the shower. For a minute I think of the bathroom at home, dingy roses on the shower curtain and how my mom would've been in there this morning, left the sink wet and her toothbrush out. I would've cleaned it up before school if I was there, but I'm not. Without me the mess will accumulate, a toothbrush here, a towel there, uncapped shampoo, a week before it gets big enough for her to notice anything is different or missing. I mean obviously she knows I'm gone, she probably even called the cops or some boyfriend, but it'll take a while before she sees it makes a difference. As long as she still has her guys and dreams of Disneyland or something like it, it doesn't really matter where I am.

Which by now is in a white tile bathroom halfway between bus-station bathroom and McDonald's, anonymous, mildew smell barely camouflaged by bleach, walls lined with those fake mirrors you can't really see yourself in. The shower is Quarters Only and all I've got left is bills and nickels, so I wash my face with paper towels and head to the front desk for change.

Whoever works it is apparently on lunch, and when I

walk outside to find a 7-Eleven there's this Tracy person squatted down and smoking beneath the Spearmint Rhino billboard. "Hey," she says. "I saw you watching me last night." The way she's squinting I think she might hit me or something.

I pretend not to know what she's talking about and chew my thumbnail. "What?" is what I muster.

"I saw you watching me. When I came in with Critter."

"Critter?"

"Yeah, the guy I was with? Whatever. It's rude to stare."

It's funny: there she is, squatted down, grimy-nailed, sucking ash through a filterless cigarette, patches on her black chained pants full of foul language—and she's telling me about manners. "You don't look like you care much about rude," I say, and as soon as it's out of my mouth I start thinking what I'd do if she gets mad. Really she's not that different from all the dirtball bully boys in Ludlow, I tell myself, and I stand up for myself with them all right.

But she just grins at me. "Yeah," she says. She looks like a wet rat when she smiles. "That's true." I just stand there, half smirking, not sure if it's cool or not to smile back. "Got a buck twenty-nine? I could use a taco," she says, and offers me a cigarette. I ask her for a light.

After that Tracy's my de facto best friend in Los Angeles. I say de facto because there aren't any others, which makes her automatically the best, but secretly even if there were she'd be my favorite. She's not like anybody on TV or back in Ludlow. She doesn't give a shit about my straight A's either, but she cares even less about pretty, and she wants to know about the words that buzz around inside my head. She's real, the first real thing I've ever met, and she scares me just a little. Nobody's ever scared me before.

Tracy knows lots of people besides me, but they're all guys with names like Critter and Squid who hang out on the sidewalk with a pit bull and spend their money on 40s. I'm pretty sure they all want to get in her pants, so none of them is really her friend.

Right away they start in asking who's the goody-goody, meaning me. Tracy always keeps us out on the edge of the group, only talking to Critter, but I can still hear them. I don't dress like them in black jeans and once-white-now-brown wifebeaters, rags and patches, spikes and bleach. My clothes come from Wal-Mart in Ludlow; it's not like I've got money to spend looking punk. My hair is brown, not green or dreadlocked orange, and I don't hustle or shoot up. They call me Country Girl and holler things at Tracy. She never says much to them except fuck off, and they always just keep talking.

But she goes back to Critter every couple days around sunset, finds him by the 7-Eleven or the alley, stands just in eyeshot till he leaves the pack and comes to her. I stick to her side till he pulls her over by the Dumpsters and I'm left there, shuffling, while Scabius yells shit at me from twenty feet away. When she comes back I breathe relief and take her to Benito's Taco Shop, home of the famous rolled taco. She likes red beans or sometimes chicken.

Besides Benito's, we spend a lot of time at the donut shops around Santa Monica and Vine. Twin Donut, Fancy Donut, Tang's Donut, Winchell's. Twin has the best coffee but they kick us out faster than the others; they have a one-hour limit. Sometimes when the cops come in and check her out Tracy gets antsy and tells me "Let's get out of here," and I follow her even though I don't have any reason to be scared of cops. Nobody's looking for me.

The day Tracy tells me about her dad, we've been kicked out of Twin Donut and cops have shown up at Tang's to try and talk to her; we didn't stick around long enough to find out what they wanted. So we're reduced to hanging out at Winchell's, the lowest rung on the donut ladder. They've got a special: two donuts and a jumbo coffee, and I eat the donuts while she drinks. I almost never see her hungry.

The thing that gets me is how matter-of-fact she is. I mean, it's not like I expect her to cry or something; she never does and besides I know enough to know that after a while you dry up. But it's more than not crying: she sounds like a news anchor, the way her voice loses its edges and she reports the facts. No details, just facts, like she's telling the story of someone else and doesn't know their insides, the way things smell and feel.

It started when she was ten. She never told her mom. First he just came in sometimes past bedtime; by six months later he split her open every other night. After five years she snuck out and didn't leave a note. She had a sister, who'd be ten about now. Sometimes at night around bedtime she thought of hitching home, breaking a window and stealing her back.

I want to ask her why didn't she do it. I'd go with her if she wanted, we could cut the screens together. I had a knife. I look at her looking down at the Formica table and I can see it, us up on Cahuenga by the on-ramp, thumbs out, headed east into too-bright sunrise, squinting it out till we hit the desert and dust got in our mouths. We'd plot out our plan of action like a couple of spies, get in and out of the house without even leaving handprints. I'd help her; I'd know how once we were there.

It's quiet at our table for a minute, inside the sound of donut orders and where's the sugar for the coffee and a drunk guy muttering in the back about new shoes and socks. Nobody's ever told me something like that before. Something real. I watch Tracy pick at her fingernails, scrape dirt from under them like she knows they'll never really be clean. I want to ask her why doesn't she do it, go home, get her sister, and I try to think of how to say it without sounding like I think I know something, because I don't. The quiet swells while I try to think of ways to say things till finally she drains her coffee and stands up. "I gotta go," she says. "Critter's waiting for me at Benito's." I want to tell her to wait, give me one more minute and I'll have something to say, but I don't. I just trail her out the door and back onto the street.

Somehow we never wind up at that Winchell's again, and I never can bring up her dad. It makes that day a bubble, contained in itself and fragile. Sometimes I look at her and I can feel it: the Formica of the table, sick-sweet of coconut donuts, the bitter black of sludgy coffee and the glare of buzzing light, all tucked in a pocket inside me. In that bubble she's still saying things nobody knows and I'm still wordless, not knowing how to fill the space she opened up, but wanting to and watching her and staying with her after, following her so she'll know that I won't leave. The bubble edge around that day makes it not just a memory but a secret, and I hold on to it like I could keep it safe. When the boys show up and Tracy switches seats to sit with Critter I roll it over in my mouth, rub it in my fingers like a stone and think: You guys will never touch this.

Critter isn't Tracy's boyfriend. I don't know how I found that out really; I just know after a while, the way you know a place, the way it smells, the angles and the corners. Sometimes she goes and meets him or talks to him off on the edges where I can't hear, but that's all. She never talks about him when he isn't there.

Still it makes me mad when she leaves me to meet him.

She always comes back quiet, neck stiff from slouching, and won't look me in the eye. It takes me an hour of sitting there not asking questions before she'll start talking again.

Once I tried to ask her where they'd gone and her eyes went slitty. Right then she reminded me of a coyote I'd seen in a petting zoo when I was nine. Everything else was baby goats and sheep and cows, and there was this coyote in a chicken-wire cage, trying to find a place to hide. But there was nowhere to go so it just stood there, backed into the corner of the cage it was trapped in, and watched the people point at it. Tracy was like that right then, and I felt like a kid with my fists full of petting-zoo food.

After that I never ask her where they've been or where she came from. It kind of makes it magic: she disappears and then shows up again like someone waved a wand. I still feel something knot up underneath my chest when she leaves, though. I guess it's what people call jealous. I've never cared about anyone enough to be jealous before, and even though the inside of my chest is crawling, I also kind of love her more that she could make me feel that way.

To make the time she's gone pass quicker, I start walking. I never get farther than Alameda on the north end or Olympic on the south, and other than Burbank I never leave Hollywood. I know there's way more of the city spread out beyond those edges, enough to wear out three pairs of shoes if I tried to walk it all. But I kind of don't want to. I like the feeling of knowing it goes beyond what I could see or touch or travel, always more out there somewhere. There are all these names I've heard but still can't picture: Brentwood, Inglewood, Glendale, Echo Park. I want to keep the words inside my head and the places unfamiliar. It leaves open the possibility that one of the places inside the names is magic. Even if I know it isn't true, at least then I can't prove it isn't.

Inside that cross-street box, though, I go everywhere: down Sunset, up Highland, on La Brea toward the fenced-off tar pits. I spend a lot of time on the tourist strip of Hollywood Boulevard, by the shops that sell pictures of celebrities left over from the '80s. The falafel is cheap there and it's one of two stretches of street I've found where people actually walk around. Tracy taught me to panhandle so I wouldn't use up all my savings, and most places it's pretty hopeless, with the strangers closed inside their air-conditioned cars. But that part of Hollywood is full of people, and Wisconsin Kansas Utah tourists all feel guilty when they see the TV-movie runaway out on the street begging for change. They think if they flip me a quarter they'll stave off my descent into the naked grainy-video underbelly of the city, so they always drop their change and keep on walking.

Lots of people keep on walking in L.A. Or driving, but either way it's the same: they look forward and keep moving past. The strip-mall signs draw your eye up and out, away from what's happening at street level, near your own skin, and you just thread through it all, keep the blinders on, wind in your ears. Sitting on the sidewalks I see it over and over. One time I'm coming out of the 7-Eleven when a little girl falls on the concrete. She must be about six, just trips and falls like six-year-olds do, scrapes her grubby knees and starts crying. Her junkie-skinny dad just keeps on walking. But she won't follow. She's still little enough to know when something hurts you don't get up and walk away from it, so she sits there till he comes back.

When he does he still won't touch her, though, or talk. Just slouches over her scraped-knee sobs and lets her cry, staring at the sidewalk or I don't know what. Finally I get in front of him, squat down and ask her "Are you okay?" She skitters behind his skeleton legs and clings to his acid-washed jeans, staring out at me through dirt and snot and tears. He doesn't move. His eyes are like the wax museum. "Man, give your kid a hug," I say. "She's crying. Just hug her. It'll fix it." He looks through me like I'm only a voice, but bends down and puts his hand on the edge of her shoulder. He doesn't even really touch her, just the air around her, like he thinks her skin will hurt him. It doesn't make her stop crying at all.

He's so skinny and his eyes are dead; it'd be so easy to shove him out of the way so I could grab that girl and hold her. But she cowers behind him like I'm a thing she needs to be protected from. Like he'll protect her. After a while he pulls her up by the armpit and keeps on walking again. She stumbles to catch up to him, says "Daddy, Daddy," still thinking he might hear her.

All day after I watch them walk away I hold that girl inside my head.

When Tracy comes back later I tell her about them. "Motherfucker," she says. "We should go find that fucking guy and take his daughter and raise her ourselves." And I know if we could find them that she'd do it. That's why I love Tracy. I could never tell her but I know she's just like that little girl, with her ratty hair and grimy weasel face and skittery eyes. But she quit clinging to the skeleton legs of the daddy that didn't touch her right, wiped the snot off her cheeks and learned to look strangers straight in the face. That's why I love her.

I want to say *Well come on then, let's go get a flashlight and troll through the streets till we find them, smoke out every house in L.A. so they're forced into the outside where we can see them, take that girl and grab her in our arms and run.* But I know that it can't happen so I don't. Instead I say "Let's get a taco."

When we're a block from Benito's I see that Critter and the guys are there. I want to tell her that I changed my mind, I want donuts instead. But they already saw us. As we walk the last few yards I hold my breath, hoping Tracy won't get sucked into Critter-world and leave me waiting for our food. But when we get there Tracy just marches to the counter, orders red beans and rice, and asks me for two dollars. It's only a dollar thirty-seven but I let her pocket the change.

We're about to take off when Scabius asks me for a blowjob. Actually he doesn't ask; he tells me to give him one or get off their piece of sidewalk. It rolls out of his mouth easy, like he's asking for spare change, but then he lets it hang there, won't let me pass it by. Critter laughs and no one else says anything and Scabius goes "Well, how about it, Country Girl?" I can feel the corner I'm backed into even in the open air of sidewalk and the seconds stretch out like they do when you're stuck in fight-or-flight and can't do either one. My face gets hot. I can't look at Tracy. She could go either way, I think: leave me to fend for myself like her sister or search me out and save me like the scraped-knee sidewalk stranger girl. These guys have been there longer than me.

After just about forever Tracy says "Fuck you." It comes out like ice, or glass, or steel. When I turn around her eyes aim past me like I'm not even there. "Don't pull that shit, you fucking coward," she says, and spits on the sidewalk at his feet. A little of it flies off and hits him. It looks like she's not quite finished, like she wants to say something else; her jaw clenches and she's pointing something at him sharper than any knife I've ever seen. His face turns pink through the orange of his freckles. She's skinnier and stragglier than all those guys, a little dried-out weed against the wind of them, but there is something in her fierce enough to change her size. It whittles her down till she's skeleton-small, swells her up till she fills the whole street, all at the same time like Alice, and her edge turns sharp and scary. Scabius stares at her and she stares back, so hard it seems like it could hurt him, her eyes bigger than themselves and drilling through the air. I've never seen Tracy talk to Scabius before, and I've never seen her look like this. Squid keeps his gaze on them but doesn't say anything; Rusty can't watch. The air's thick and the silence is loud; it seems like someone might get hurt even though no one's doing anything but talking. It's enough to make Critter say "Yeah, come on, man, let it go," and then the rest of them fall like dominoes and the air thins.

Nobody's ever sworn for me before, let alone changed size. I want to say thank you, but she won't look at me.

The rest of that day Tracy's as silent as she is about her dad since that day that we talked, and I know not to ask if she's going to still hang around with Critter and those guys or what. But part of me wonders if maybe that was it, if she took sides and now she'll stick to her story. I want it to be true too much to ask.

But that night up on Hollywood her eyes start moving around again. She goes and gets me a falafel, looks at the sidewalk, and tells me she's got an errand to run. I know what that means: Critter. It makes my stomach this weird yellow sort of sick, and I don't know whose side it puts me on, but I breathe in and say "Okay," and wait for her outside the Wax Museum.

An hour later, as sunset turns the sky orange and the buildings black, I spot Tracy headed up the block toward me, fast: head thrust up, eyes forced open. When she gets close to me I can see the blood. When she gets closer I can see her cheek is turning purple. He did that to her. "Oh shit," I say, and run the rest of the way, and when I get to her I pull her into my chest without thinking, hard, a scraped-knee girl with nobody to hide behind. She stumbles, surprised, and for a second I get scared I've backed her in a corner and she's about to bolt. I don't want her to run, so I don't ask her anything. I shut my mouth and close my eyes and she lets me hold her there, like that, as the sun sinks down behind us.

The next morning she says she'll be right back and looks me straight in the face, no shifty eyes. I don't ask where she's going, but the way she looks at me I can tell she'll come right back. She walks off south and half an hour later comes back grinning, grabs me by the arm, and says "I'm finished with that motherfucker. No more Critter. Take me someplace else."

We walk north, away from Benito's and the hostel, the

donut shops on Santa Monica, to places she hasn't been before: the Church of Scientology with its polished halls full of drones with weirdo glassy eyes, La Brea Tar Pits set up like Prehistoric Land with plastic mammoths, the L.A. River up in Burbank where you can scale the railings, drop down and walk the asphalt banks for miles. Two nights in a row we hike to the observatory and sleep where the hills open up, skyline blends into stars, and it glitters till the light lulls you to sleep. All the places I went while she was off with Critter I take her to, and all of them are better with her there.

The third morning she gets antsy, though, and calls it homesick. She starts smoking lots of cigarettes and says the city feels too big, like it could swallow her. She promises that she won't talk to him, won't leave again, but could we head back down there, just for a day or two, where the side-walks are familiar? I've never figured her to be a small-town type like that, nervous when the world reminds you that it's bigger than you'll ever know, but I know what she means. Some nights I miss the strip of road outside my house in Ludlow, and I feel it too. I swallow the hot doubt clumped in my throat and say okay.

Over the next few days the antsy gets worse. She's out of money, that's part of it; but there's something else too, an edge that keeps her broke because nobody will stop to give her anything. Even the trannie prostitutes turn their backs to

her when she tries to go and talk to them. I start buying cigarettes so I'll have some the second she runs out; when I don't
have any she starts pacing parking lots, looking to bum them
from strangers. They get scared of the size-shifting glint in
her eyes and she barks at them, swears at their backs as they
walk away. It embarrasses me. She bites her nails till her fingers are bloody, and sometimes when she thinks I'm asleep I
can hear her cry. She doesn't want to leave our stretch of
Sunset but she can't sit still, won't stay in one place; she seems
like she's looking for something but she'll never say what.

She stays by my side, though. Every time she goes someplace
new, which is about every ten minutes, she brings me with
her. Come on, she'll say. Let's go to Winchell's or Tang's or
the Dollar Chinese by El Centro. Never back to 7-Eleven,
the alley, or Benito's, though. Not back to those guys.

    I follow her, of course. I think if I just stay near her and
don't talk too much I can see her through whatever tunnel
she's in, and be there at the end of it when she wants to be
pulled out. I think maybe I could be some kind of light. It's
funny that I think that, considering what I've known since I
was ten about the way the city grimes you, how the dirt dulls
out anything you were trying to find that was shiny. I guess
I must think we're exempt.

We're at a Winchell's when I see that we're not. It's not the
Winchell's where she told me about her dad, but they all

look the same inside, remind me of the bubble of that day. Somehow I figure if she trusted me once at those yellow tables, maybe she'll do it again. She's been shaking all morning but it's starting to subside, and once I even say something that makes her laugh and snort black coffee out her nose. I'm eating crullers which I put between us on the table so she knows that she can have some if she wants.

In the middle of a sentence she stands up to hit the bathroom. That part is normal; she's got a bad stomach, she says, and I'm used to her running off to deal with it. What isn't normal is that on the way back, wiping water off her mouth, she bends down to talk to this comb-over guy at the back table who's been watching us. She never talks to strangers. Lots of them try; guys mostly, all older. I always just ignore them but Tracy fends them off, makes clever cutting comments I always wish I thought of. But this guy tugs at her shirt as she passes him and when she turns around, ready to fight, he says something that makes her stop. I can see the conversation: she asks him something, he makes some kind of offer, she bites her lip and thinks. I squint to read their lips and frown hard straight at Tracy, try to pull her back to our table like a magnet.

She does, finally, but with a switch in her hips that looks weird against her skinny weasel body. He follows her. He takes Tracy's seat across from me; she squeezes in next to him. He's sweaty and yellow and smells like old grease. He picks up a cruller and eats it in about five seconds. I hate him.

Tracy is acting polite, which I've never seen. She's like my mom around her boss, with the same sweet stilted way of talking my mom always calls Being Professional. It's bizarre. Tracy introduces the comb-over guy as Rob-He's-a-Director. She says he has a job for us, if we want it, and since we're so broke she thought . . . He cuts in and says "I'm paying your friend Tracy in candy, but she said you wouldn't want it so I'm prepared to give you cash. That way it works for both of you." He smiles at me all slick and friendly in a way that's not friendly at all. Tracy looks at her lap. I know what candy is.

I could tell you that all of a sudden it all makes sense, the bitten fingernails, the stomach, the shakes; the jumpy-eyed swearing at strangers and the way Critter wasn't Tracy's boyfriend but she always, always left with him. I could tell you that it all makes sense, but the truth is that it doesn't. It comes together, sure, in a way that makes the facts line up, provides an explanation. But it doesn't make sense at all.

I sit there while he keeps on talking, goes on and on describing the setup and how it would work, how little we'd actually have to do, how basically it's just taking our clothes off and that's not so bad now is it, and I'm up on the white tile ceiling, pressed up against the blackened mildew in the cracks and looking down at Tracy looking down, her face in her lap, and she won't ever ever raise her eyes to look at me. I can see the whole room, everyone with their faces on their laps or hands or donuts, everyone just walking by, driving by, moving through, eyes like the wax museum, blinders on. All these people falling down and scraping knees and everyone just forging ahead, afraid to touch anything but the air around each other, and it isn't enough, it doesn't make anyone stop crying at all.

I tell Tracy I love her. In my periphery I see Rob the Director get cagey, calculate me as a risk. But he's far away, out at the corners of things, unreal. I switch size like Alice, and as fast as my vision had spread to hold the whole room, now it shrinks like a pinned pupil tight on Tracy. I tell Tracy I love her and I tell her look at me, lift her chin up and look at my eyes. I'll help you, I say, I know how and I'll do it. I'll come and get you like your sister or that girl on the sidewalk, take you, keep you safe, make you stop crying. I know how. I put my hand on hers and hold it, tight so I can feel the bones, the blood, the lines in her palm. She's shaking again.

It would be so easy to lay into Rob, tell him to fuck off and spit at his feet, scare him away from both of us. But Tracy's moved in so close to Rob she's almost hidden behind his skinny greasy shoulder, like I'm a thing she needs to be protected from. Here I am saying that I love her, holding her hand past the air around her and down to the bones, and she's cowering behind this stranger bearing candy.

"Tracy?" I say, finally asking for an answer. I know the risks of asking Tracy questions. I know she could point her caged-coyote face at me, turn quick and testy behind the eyes, swear at me or spit. I know I'm drawing a line down the middle and making her choose, risking that she'll bolt and burst our bubble. But I don't have a choice. She's so far away right now that if I don't ask she'll slip out of sight. I ask her the question. She shakes her head at her lap, inches in closer to Rob. She's taken sides; now she'll stick to her story.

It's funny how it all still looks the same out the car window. Somewhere in that tangle of city Tracy's probably painted up in some grainy-video basement, playing out the TV-movie myth; and looking from the outside you'd think it was scary or sad enough to change the landscape, but it's not. The signs are the same, MEL'S and HOLLYWOOD perched on the fault lines, withstanding the earthquakes of what can happen to one person here, and I'm watching from another set of windows in another car, and nothing looks much different.

I don't think that places change you. They're too fixed, too solid to do much of anything. The things that really change you are the things that change themselves: ground opening up along a fault and gulping down your house, people picking sides, their answers to your questions. Tracy changed me and I still don't understand it. She's land that split and swallowed parts of me; no matter how hard I press the sides together the crack won't close, the pieces won't click back into place.

I never say good-bye that day. I say I love you one more time and walk out of Winchell's, keep walking till I hit Highland which turns into Cahuenga by the 101. It's easier to get a ride this time: I can tell which cars to hold my thumb out for and which ones will just keep driving. I know how to spot the blinders now, and I don't try to get the passersby to look my way. I just wait to see a set of eyes that's still open, unfixed, who'll stop and take me north, past home and out of Hollywood, beyond what I can see or touch or travel, toward names I've always heard but never seen.

tracy

i could list for you the places I've been: Reno. Vegas.
Bakersfield San Bernardino Riverside. None of them is
home and I always come back to L.A., which isn't home
either, it just knows me. I could tell you how it feels to hitch
through desert till your eyes bleed from dust and you bruise
your toes kicking dirt, how the rigs pull through like shiny
metal monsters, windshields shielding the creeps inside and
you hate each truck for being shiny and purple and bigger
than you but when they slow down you climb in and then
you're part of it and moving.

I could tell you the names of everyone I've known or
tricked or slept with, but they all leave anyway or I do and
besides I quit keeping track really. There are lots of things
I've known and done but when you're standing on a sidewalk in the city you always leave and then come back to and
it's still not home, your history is like an itchy phantom
limb: you can feel it, but it isn't really there.

I could tell you all this shit and probably you'd like it,

but I won't. Suffice it to say I'm on the sidewalk by the St. Moritz Hotel, Sunset past the 101, eleven thirty or so in the morning on a Tuesday, and I'm waiting for Rob. Rob is my director. He has bad skin and gooped-up combed-over hair and wears his acid-wash like it's still 1988. He drives a '91 Civic and is always on time to pick me up. We hit House of Pies sometimes, other times IHOP; the old-lady waitresses scowl, I eat my eggs, and then we go to work.

I am Rob's star, which I think is hilarious. He calls me that: his star, his leading lady. He positions other girls around me like I'm some sun and they're orbiting, pretending he's some bigwig who "assembles girls." Really he brings them in when they're strung out, pissed off and cold. Whichever ones show up on his stretch of sidewalk are the ones who get brought up to his studio on the outer fringes of Toluca Lake, and I'm the star because I'm always there. But he'd have you think that was the plan from the start.

I've gotten used to it: now it's just another condition, like heat, cold, wet jeans. After a while you stop noticing the camera, the parade of dry-eyed junkie girls gets regular, you see yourself in all of them. It's normal. The first time it was weird, though, like the first time of anything is weird, and you suck in and breathe through it and it's over soon and added to the list of things you are. The naked-for-a-stranger part was fine, crossed that bridge long before, but the camera got under my skin, comb-over Rob with his acid-wash yelling out instructions, the fat girl who batted sleepy eyes at me and wouldn't talk. The whole thing was too planned out, too much of a production, more like a television show or the Superbowl than what I was used to (old lonely guys in rooms). Too much icing. The effort of it all was pathetic, I preferred the tragic grandpas, the camera made me sick; but what was I going to do, complain? Rob had drugs.

Ah, drugs. I could tell you about those too, but you know already. For a while they spice things up or blot them out, make it better or at least extra; it's you using them, and then it becomes the other way around. That's all it is. Just another puppet string pulling at your elbows, making you move. At first I fought it, swore to quit, jaw set, but after a few go-rounds I realized it was like trying to quit being hungry. I never had the willpower to be anorexic. There's only so much you can transcend. So I got skinny the easy way, ha-ha.

The rest of them never come up by the St. Moritz. They all stay down on Santa Monica by Benito's, Critter and Rusty and Germ and fucking Scabius, probably Laura too. I've been around those kids a bunch of months, since I rolled into L.A. the last time; they're the closest thing to family I've got, which still isn't very close. Once I shift five blocks up and three blocks over I'm as good as out of town to them.

It didn't have to be like that. When Rob first asked me to work, I tried to get Laura to come with me. I figured it was a deal for both of us: she had zero clue how to make money out here, being from Ludlow or wherever; I needed the junk and wasn't about to go back to Critter for it. Plus we could do it together, which would make the whole thing more fun.

It'd been like that—together and more fun—for two weeks already, since she showed up at the hostel all fresh-faced in clean clothes with her Wal-Mart backpack, pony-tailed brown hair, a brand-spanking-new runaway. Freckles, even. Pretty quick it was just me and her: at the Dollar Chinese, Tang's Donut, spare-changing up on Hollywood. Company, and I didn't even have to fuck her. I'd never had that, not in San Bernie or Bakersfield, sure as hell not back in Nevada. I mean I always had someone, but only with a trade-off. You always have to fuck someone or take care of them or buy them shit, and if you don't they walk away.

Laura didn't want anything from me, though; that part was new, and it put us on the same side of things. Compadres, or whatever. So when comb-over Rob showed up like some greasy angel to find me four days clean, shaking and puking in the donut-store bathroom, I figured Laura and me were all set.

Rob'd been courting me almost a month now, at this Winchell's and the one off Vine, eyeing me when I wasn't with Critter, asking if he could help me with anything. He was pretty nasty, with these forehead pimples I was just about dying to pop, even though he was clearly way past thirty and should've outgrown his zits a long fuckin' time ago. I never wanted shit to do with Rob: I had Critter, my knight in crusty armor, who gave me junk like it was roses and he was my boyfriend or some fuckin' thing. Pretty easy, as far as trade-offs go. Kind of luxurious, even, till he broke my fuckin' cheekbone.

Back when Critter was around, Rob would try to touch my sleeve and I'd stare him down; my eyes went straight through like they were a power drill and he was paper. Just another greased-up weedy sidewalk cat who wanted ass. I wouldn't talk to him. But I'd gone kind of AWOL these three days since Critter punched me. I wasn't about to be the girl who lets herself get hit for drugs; that shit gets around quick, and before you know it you're getting gang-banged in some Taco Bell bathroom. That, and I had no other source. I was sick as hell, my fever dreams kept me from sleeping, and I couldn't tell Laura about the junk or she'd get scared and run away. I was fucked.

So this day was Rob's lucky one, I guess, and mine. I normally wouldn't work for someone else, but if me and Laura were a team I figured we would both be safe.

I guess Laura didn't see it that way, though. Instead she just stared at me like I was a TV set till Rob stopped talking, and then pulled this shit of saying she loved me in the middle of fucking Winchell's Donut, over two crullers, in front of Rob, and taking off. It didn't make any sense; why she would do that and then go. I mean, it made sense that she'd go; someone always does. But I don't know why she had to say she loved me. If she loved me, whatever the fuck that meant, she'd be with me: in Rob's Civic, headed up Ventura toward the Valley.

But no, so now I was by myself again, surprise, thighs sticking to the ripped red leather vinyl of the seat, no a/c in the car of course, just a crappy fan spitting stale air through the plastic vents into my eyes. Rob kept trying to talk to me, find out where I was from and who my parents were, small talk, that kind of shit. I told him I came from a family of Gypsies in France. He narrowed his eyes at me like he was weighing whether or not to believe it and then spat out the window. His spit was white and stringy like an egg. It blew back on the glass behind him and stuck there, quivering in the wind.

Here is the order it goes in with Rob: eat, shoot a scene, then drugs. My first day he had me do one scene after another after another, different other girls, positions, scenarios. For some Internet thing, he said. He worked me till I was dried out and my skin stung, eyes pulled out of focus by the sharp of the fluorescents, mouth sour. I was too freaked out to protest, locked in his concrete warehouse with no ride to pick me up, and I didn't know if he was the type to use a knife or what.

But at the end he kept his promise and then let me go, so when I came back two days later I knew what I was dealing with and I laid it out. One scene, then I got paid. If he wanted more, okay, but I got to shoot up after every one. That way I could just lay back. Plus he would get me a room at the St. Moritz, by the week, which he wasn't allowed to come into ever. And some shit to take home with me, to last me till the next day, every time. He got all ruffled, puffed out his skinny chest like we were birds, but I knew he wasn't any bigger than me. "This is a business transaction," I told him. "You want my business?" And of course he did.

Now it's been four weeks of this. Some nights I stay up there at his warehouse in Toluca Lake, when I'm too stoned to take the ride down to the St. Moritz. But mostly I go back to my room and eat Chinese food, I guess like grown-ups when they go home after work. Which is weird because I'm not a grown-up, and Hollywood isn't home.

I never sleep in alleys anymore. I don't have to: I've got sheets now and a bed and a lock on the door, all paid for. Critter always wanted that: our own room, a little home. He'd talk about it like it would change things, like it would keep us safe and make us real. I knew that wasn't ever true, but I'd go along with it because it felt good just to watch someone believe something. Sometimes I think about going down to Benito's to find him, bring him up here, lock the door behind us. But I can't. He'd ask me who was paying for the room.

And anyway, I'm not running after any of those guys.

No way I'm chasing after Scabius's nasty face or Critter's fist. No one came looking for me when I left. Rusty's the only person who ever came to find me, and that was way back in Venice when he didn't have anybody else and he was broke. No one looks for you unless they need something. And I don't need anything from them.

So it's eleven thirty on a Tuesday and I'm outside the St. Moritz. Rob pulls up before I'm finished with my cigarette, which is a good excuse to make him wait. He sits in the Civic watching me, jittery, and I can tell he's tapping his foot down by the brake pedal. Cops come around here all the time, as if it would actually make a difference, and even though I told Rob I'm eighteen, I know he knows I'm not.

I smoke it down to the filter before I stub it out. When I get in the car I can taste the fiberglass. I run my tongue over my teeth. Rob hands me half a soda; the wet sweaty cup feels like it might crumple and spill Fanta in my lap, but I drink it anyway. He seems nervous: I can feel it even looking out the window.

He's got someone special for me today, he says. Oh goody. No, he says, he thinks I'll really like her, but I have to promise not to give her a hard time. I don't know why he cares; it all looks the same on his crappy webcam anyway, but he insists. No, he says, he means it: he wants me to promise. I look at him. His eyes are off the road and on me.

"Okay," I go. "I promise."

The traffic on the 101 is like a snarl in your hair: it seems like it'll be tangled in itself forever but if you keep on pressing eventually it loosens up and lets you through. When we get close to the warehouse Rob starts talking again. "We're late," he says, "and she'll probably be scared." I look at him like, *And so?*

"She's young, okay?" he goes. "That's why I want you to be nice."

"I thought you only worked with girls who were over eighteen," I say, just to give him shit.

"Oh, shut up," he goes.

We pull up onto the gravel and park. Before I can grab my backpack and get out, Rob reaches over and smoothes my hair around my face. He seems awkward, like he doesn't really know how to touch a person. I flinch.

When he's satisfied with my hairstyle he says "Okay," and we get out. He goes in ahead of me, flips on the light and starts talking to someone. I can hear their voices, but I'm in no rush. I stay by the door and light a smoke, watching guys go in and out of the auto-body place across the street. They look like ants.

I'm only halfway done when Rob sticks his head out the door. "Tracy," he whispers so loud he might as well talk regular, "come on. We're waiting for you in here."

I take one last drag. "You got my shit?" I ask him. I'm

supposed to get it from him after but he asked me to act nice, so I figure he better do something extra for me too. It's only fair.

He looks at me for a second, between thoughts, like his brain is stuttering. Then he says "Yeah, hang on" and goes inside.

After a second he comes back out with it, hands me the keys, and tells me to go do it in the car. "What the fuck?" I ask him. But he says "Just go," and it'd take too much work to argue.

He waits by the passenger side. Numb and sleepy, I hand him the keys when I get out and follow him inside. I finger the shit I've got left over, a tinfoil pebble in my pocket. "Be nice," he whispers through his teeth as we walk through the door.

Inside the light is dim, not buzzing white fluorescent like usual. It matches the feeling in my body but it makes me have to blink. Everything is blurry and dark for a minute while my pupils adjust.

Then I see her.

It's weird how when you see someone in a place you don't expect, your brain won't believe it's actually them. There's this pause while my brain separates out from my body, and it's like I'm in a movie and watching it, both at the same time. Then it snaps back like a rubber band.

"Eeyore," I go. "What the fuck are you doing here?"

She was chubby before, but now her clothes dangle

off her like a hanger. She's got all this makeup on: mascara raccooning her eyes, blending into the circles underneath, blush on her cheeks like a doll. Her lip ring is crusty and her hair's grown out so the top half is brown and the bottom half's purple. She smiles when she sees me in this sort of dazed way, eyes wide but too soft to be crazy. I don't know if she's high or what. She doesn't answer me.

"*Eeyore,*" I say again, harder, making sure she heard me. Rob watches us back and forth like Ping-Pong. She just stands there. I run outside and throw up.

It's forty-five minutes from Toluca Lake to Hollywood, and that's one ride with no traffic. Hitching, it takes me almost three hours. By the time I get back to the St. Moritz I'm out of cigarettes, my eyes are sore and I'm starving.

I wish there was a shower in my room, or even a sink: my face is crawling and sticky, my hands thick with dried sweat. But the bathroom's down the hall, so I just wrap myself up in the yellow-stained sheets and hope they'll rub off the dirt.

I try really hard to fall asleep. I can tell it isn't gonna happen. I do a little of the junk I've got left over, but it's not enough to really calm me down. My blood's still racing and my skin's awake and prickly and I can't stop thinking about Eeyore.

I don't know why I give a shit. I mean, it's weird: you'd think I'd want someone I know there with me. I did with

Laura. But Eeyore's young. She looks even younger with the weight off, like some skinny starving kid, the kind you see in pictures of other countries. Like me. She never looked like me before.

I lie on the mattress a long time, eyes closed, heart pounding, before I finally drift off. Even then it's the kind of sleep that's only on the surface, skimming the tops of your thoughts while your mind's still working underneath. I know the feeling from when I used to sleep outside. Even if you dream, it just feels like you're thinking.

Underneath the thin skin of dark we curl up in my bed like spoons, me and my baby sister Ruthanne. The room is blue and I can't see, but I know it's her: her hands are small like little kitten paws and her hair smells soft like baby sweat and laundry. It feels like corn silk on my lips. The dark is like a fort made of blankets, an envelope holding me inside. I've been in this exact same place before.

Light splits the door and then a shadow takes up everything. His big body gets between us, rough and hard like rocks: the baby smell goes and my nose fills with thick hot black air, so dirty I can't breathe. My teeth hurt like something cracked them; I taste blood. And then I'm gone, fast, somewhere up near the ceiling, and the air opens up again.

I know Ruthanne's air won't open up, though. Not without me. She's stuck there in the black rough sludge with him; she's too little to get out. If I made myself sink I could stretch down and drag her up to the ceiling, and then she could breathe in too. But I don't. I stay up above them where it's cool and watch her drown.

The next morning the feeling of that dream stays in me way after I wake up and all I want is to watch TV or talk to someone, but I can't. I don't go meet Rob. I stay up in my room through ten thirty and eleven thirty and even on to one. It isn't easy: last time I ate was breakfast yesterday, and I barely have enough junk left over to keep from getting sick. But I don't want to see him. Actually, that's wrong: I don't care if I see him or not. I don't want to see her.

Without me there he can't keep her more than a couple days: there's only so much one girl can do by herself, and I know he's too protective of her to bring some stranger in. When they run out of options he'll just send her away and make sure he knows where he can find her later. All I have to do is wait him out.

By two I'm sure Rob's given up on waiting for me in the parking lot and I go down the ratty stairs. Outside the sun is way too bright, even through the smog; it forces my eyes open, pries my pupils wide. I don't have any money.

Up on Hollywood it takes me half an hour to spange enough for a falafel. Hot sauce burns through my nose and I forget to chew. After I wipe my hands I realize I don't have any place to go or anyone to go with. It's the first time that's happened in six months at least; it's weird. For a minute I remember finding Eeyore in her school parking lot where I was selling weed; and then my first night sleeping out with her, how she trusted me to find a place for us to lie down safe, the stars reflected on her little-kid face, and then I push it away. I don't even know why I remember that.

I figure as long as there's nothing to do I might as well stay here a while with the change cup out. You never know. Eventually some guilty mom will feel so shitty for ignoring her own kids that she'll flip me a buck, or some tourist will toss a quarter so he can say he did a good deed in the big city. You can see the "There but for the grace of God" in their eyes, those few that actually look at you. And then they drop a dollar in to make the feeling go away so they can keep on walking. I lean against the hard brick of the Fantasy Sleep Wear store, watch the feet crisscross in front of me and wait.

After an hour there's four pennies in the change cup. I leave them on the sidewalk for someone to get lucky, and then start walking. I have to: without a fix or work or any-one to talk to, that dream from last night keeps rushing in to fill the space. Mostly it's the feeling of it, the blue of the room and the pull downward toward the ugly bed, the knowing you can't stop her drowning or else you'll drown yourself. My mouth tastes sick. My head fills up with corn silk and diesel fumes. I don't think of Ruthanne's face, though. I just walk.

* * *

I wait another day before it's safe to go back to work. It's hard: I keep thinking about that fucking dream, using up my little tinfoil packet bit by bit, enough to keep the cramps away but never enough to sweep me clean. I get through it knowing she'll be gone tomorrow and I can go back like normal to the eggs and junk and work and strangers, and forget again.

The next morning on my way down I feel relieved. At the bottom of the stairs Rob will be waiting: I'll see him and go back to work and just be what I'm used to, quit sitting around thinking about Eeyore and goddamn Ruthanne. I know Rob'll give me shit about the other day, me running out and hiding in my room, but it doesn't really bother me. I think I just won't answer.

He's out there waiting, pissed; he stares me down when I walk out the door. "What happened to you?" he asks. I get out a cigarette.

He asks again, though, and doesn't move to unlock the car, so I guess I have to say something. "I was sick," I tell him.

"Yeah, I guess," he goes.

"Yeah," I say. He goes around to my door to open it.

We don't eat. I guess it's my punishment for playing hooky; I don't really want to ask. On the way up to the Valley he keeps looking over at me like he's checking something. I can see him from the corner of my eye. I watch the hills out the window all the way through Burbank, the signs tucked into different shades of green, palm trees and evergreens and weird tropical shit clumping together like we're on some fucking island. I don't know how they grow in so much smog.

Eventually the ground flattens out and turns to auto-body shops and brick and wire. The tires crunch on gravel and Rob parks the car. I'm sweating and I want to ask him for my shit up front, but he doesn't owe me anything this time and I don't want to push it. More than anything I just want things to be back to normal, traded off and evened out. After I work again it will be, at least sort of. I follow Rob in through the metal front door. Once we're in he turns to me and goes "Think you can handle it this time?"

"Fuck off," I say.

Then I see what he's talking about. Eeyore's still here. She's off in the corner of the room, crouched over, picking at her nails. He's got a little area set up for her, pillows and a dirty blanket, and her backpack's stashed there too. It used to be all clean, brand-spanking new; now it's patched up, stuffed full and the zipper's broken.

She looks at me with those big wide spacey eyes; all the feeling of calm I had coming down the stairs at the St. Moritz this morning goes right away, and I don't know what the fuck I'm supposed to do. I'm pretty sure if I try to work with her I'll just throw up again, and there's this weird hollow feeling in my chest that just gets bigger the more she stares at me and doesn't talk. I keep seeing her face in the school parking lot, looking so different from the way it looks now; I want to get out of this room, back to where her eyes are the way I left them. But I can't leave. If I do, that's probably it for me with Rob, which means no more St. Moritz and no more junk from him.

It'll all at least be easier if I get fucked up, I figure, so I turn away from Eeyore and holler off for Rob. If he's gonna make me work with a twelve-year-old he can at least help me out a little. Besides, I haven't asked him for anything in three days.

"Where's my shit?" I ask when he comes strolling over. He squints like he's trying to figure me out, but I just act like it's normal. "Where is it?"

"That's not our deal," he goes. "I always give it to you after."

"And I always work with girls who aren't underage," I tell him. "It's against the law, you know." I smile.

He's massively pissed off. He knows I've got him, though. He tries to think of an argument but he can't; if I called the cops he'd be in way more trouble than me. Finally he goes "Oh, fucking fine. Just wait here half an hour. I'll be back."

"You're out?" I ask. He must've given it all to Eeyore.

"Yes, I'm fucking out. Just stay here."

"Okay," I go.

Once he slams the door behind him I turn around to Eeyore. My heart is beating really fast; it's weird. "So are you gonna talk to me?"

She just looks at me with her saucer eyes again. I can tell she's fucked up. She never used to get high and she's not handling it well; Rob probably shot her up so she'd stay. My chest feels sort of soft and sick; I just want her to say something. Finally I pick up her backpack, say "Come on" and lead her out the door.

I'm not sure where I think we're going. I don't know my way that well; I've never been around here on foot. It's just warehouses and lots, pretty much, nowhere to duck in and hide. I get us away from Rob's as fast as I can, since I know he'll be coming around in his car and if he runs into us he'll kick my ass. I don't even know what I'm doing. It's not like I'm running away; I have to go back to him for my shit eventually. I just knew Eeyore wasn't going to talk to me in there, and I couldn't stand to look at her and wonder how she got that way. I have to ask her questions.

Finally we turn about twelve corners and we're in a neighborhood of houses. Most of them are beige. There's a little alley between two yards; it's probably someone's property but it's all paved and broken glass; I'm sure no one ever comes here but cats. I pull Eeyore in and sit her down. "So what the fuck happened to you?" I ask her.

She looks up at me like she's afraid she's in trouble. "What do you mean?" she finally stutters.

"I mean, how the fuck did you wind up here?" I almost

ask her why she didn't go home when I left, but I remember the answer to that. But you'd at least think she'd have another place to go, another person to fall back on, that someone would look out for her. When cops pull up their cars near me I know they're just trying to meet their ticket quota for the day, but she's the kind of kid that's young and cute and clean enough that cops assume you've got a family, pick you up and bring you back to Child Services. The kind of kid that grown-ups care about.

"Well, after you left I couldn't go home," she says, and gives me this look like I know what she means, and I do, and she waits, like maybe I'll jump in and hold her hand or something, and I don't, so she goes on.

"I met those guys—you know, the ones we saw across the street that time—" I know she means Critter and Squid "—and then this guy Rusty started hanging out with us, and it was pretty cool for a while, and Critter, which was one of those guys across the street, was my really good friend—" and her face gets all red. "Then this asshole guy Scabius came around—" she goes.

I stop her. "What?" I ask. I can't believe it.

I can't believe a lot of things. I can't believe she's up here in the first place, and I can't believe nobody stopped for her, and I can't believe she sounds the way she does, all gravelly and scratched-up and tired and cold. I can't believe she was out on my sidewalks with everyone I knew and I didn't even know it, and I can't believe she's blushing about

Critter, and especially I can't believe she fucking hung around with Scabius. That fuck.

"Yeah, he was super mean," she says. "He had bright orange dreadlocks and a bull ring through his nose and all these freckles everywhere—"

"Yeah, I know," I say, just so she'll stop describing him.

All of a sudden her eyes get a lot less spacey. "What do you mean, you know?"

I don't feel like explaining so I just say "I've met that guy before."

"Oh," she goes, like she's expecting me to go on. I don't.

"Yeah, so him and me sort of hooked up," she finally says, her eyes on the gravel, "and then we kind of had this fight, and he told me to go home . . . I don't know." She trails off.

I just look at her. My skin is itchy and my back's starting to sweat. "Yeah?" I say.

"Yeah, but I couldn't go home. But he said to leave, so—"

"Why'd you do what he told you to?"

She looks at me with this dumb dog face, like she's never even considered she had any other option. "Umm—I don't know," she finally goes. "It was kind of like I had to."

"Why?" I ask her.

"I don't *know*," she says, and I can tell she wants me to lay off. But I don't want to. I'm not sure why. There's just this feeling pushing me: I'm mad; maybe not at her, but she's the only one around.

"Well, there must've been a reason." I sound like someone's parents.

"I don't *know*, okay?" I still don't look away. "I guess I thought if I didn't do what he said he would hurt me or something."

"*Did* he hurt you?" I ask her. Now my cheeks are hot.

"I don't know. Sort of," she says. "Plus Critter was gone—"

"Where was he?"

"I don't fucking *know*, okay? Why are you asking me all these questions?"

I can't answer. Seeing Eeyore in the first place makes me feel all soft and nervous, like an almost guilty kind of sick, and then there's this mad on top of it, this angry which isn't really at her, I don't think, but it's coming out that way. The whole thing is fucked, the way she wound up with them and then out here, so close to me, when I only knew her for a couple weeks a couple months ago. It's like she's following me or something, and I don't want her to. I want her to go somewhere else, somewhere better, away from me. But she keeps tracking me, tracing a trail back to the places that I left before. It's pissing me off. I closed a box of broken cheekbones and brick walls when I left those guys and she's opening it back up, dragging me close to them when all I want to do is get away. Especially from Scabius. I don't know what she was doing near him and I don't know what he did to her and imagining it makes me feel like I'm drowning. When she says his name I can see his ugly face inside my head and feel his nasty breath. "Whatever," I go. I don't want to fucking talk about it anymore.

I walk her back to the studio and leave before Rob gets back. I say I'm going to run an errand. I don't know where I'm going or why; I don't have a ride and I don't try to get one. I just walk: past more beige houses and concrete buildings, barbed wire and broken glass, till the lawns stop being yellow and the houses turn orange and green. They go on forever, shiny minivans in driveways, front yards full of plastic toys. The first thing you see in all the windows is the big TV. Some houses have kids in them; in one I see two girls jumping on a couch. My eyes sting.

When it starts to get dark I'm still up by Burbank but I keep walking anyway; I still don't try to get a ride. I can't stop moving. I cross over to Cahuenga and follow it down beside the 101, headed toward Hollywood, the only other place I know. My feet start to hurt and it blends in with the rest of the bad feelings in my body: I haven't shot up in almost a day. The mad feeling from before keeps rolling over itself in my head, picking up speed and size like a snowball. I'm not going to sleep tonight. The streetlight glow replaces the sun and cars start to slow down when they pass me. I keep my eyes straight ahead.

By the time I hit Franklin Ave, it must be four a.m. My stomach is growling but I'm sicker than I am hungry so I don't stop. When I hit the turnoff toward the St. Moritz I think about sheets and sleep for a second but keep going instead, down the seven blocks to Sunset, and then turn left, past the iPod billboards and the post-production suites, the construction site and Winchell's Donut, back toward Goodwill and the Dollar Chinese and Benito's, where I first brought Eeyore from her school, the other way from where I left her sleeping when I went to Venice. The sky looks the same as it did when I left her: the blackest it ever gets out here, when everything's closed but the all-night stores, and the sun hasn't started to push up from under the horizon. I waited till the darkest part of night, when there was nothing that could move and wake her up; I brought her to Whole Foods, where I knew that she'd find breakfast, and I touched her hair at sunset till her breathing changed and she was dreaming, like I used to touch Ruthanne so she could sleep no matter what would happen in the dark. I had to go. My fever dreams were starting and I couldn't find a fix to make them stop: she kept talking about her stepbrother, what he did to her, and it made me think of things I couldn't think about. There was no way I could make it stop except to get away. I knew she'd be okay. Someone would find her and take her someplace safe, or else she'd stay and be protected;

it would always be better for her than it ever was for me. She was different; she deserved it. She'd be fine without me. As long as she didn't wake up till I was gone.

I head over to Benito's like some fairy-tale lost girl, like if I follow the bread crumbs I'll get back home. Which there's no such thing as home, but I keep walking anyway. Bianca the trannie is at the counter on an orange stool, wearing leopard print, smearing lipstick on her tostada. Bianca hooked me up with junk a couple times; I haven't seen her since before I went to Venice. I keep my head down and my hoodie up and rush around the corner before she can spot me, yell "Hey, mami" at me like I'm some pretty girl. I duck into the alley.

It's dark, so it's a minute before I see them. But then a piece of metal catches the streetlight, and when I see it flash I squint to make it out, and when I do I recognize Germ's collar. I get closer. He's curled up in a ball; I count four bodies around him, all of them, Rusty and Squid and Critter and Scabius.

What I should do is turn around. What I should do is turn around and walk away and leave, go west or north, to the hotel or the beach, anywhere except here with this closed box of ugly things. But I don't. The snowball that's been rolling over itself in my head spins downhill and the mad bursts through my veins like speed, all the way out to my fingertips, and I run toward them hard and fast, not caring if I wake them up, and when I get close enough I lift my boot back and swing it into Scabius. He's sleeping on his side; I'm shooting for his balls but I get his gut instead. My steel toes curl him backward; it feels good. His eyes fly open and he tries to yell but the air's knocked out of him. Then he looks up and sees where it came from.

At first his eyes narrow and his nostrils flare, all pissed off and righteous, ready to hurt me back. But then something else crosses his face: something guilty and embarrassed, something that knows I know his secret. I smile down at him. I really feel like smiling. I cock my foot again and he flinches backward. I spit on him.

By now of course everyone else is up. Germ is panting, worst watchdog in the world, wagging his tail even though I just kicked the shit out of Scabius, and for all he knows I'm about to again. Squid's rubbing his eyes, confused. Rusty's leaned up against him, looking scared. "Hey, Tracy," he says, kind of slow, like he's not sure if he's supposed to say it or not.

Then Critter sits up and drills his eyes into me. "Tracy," he goes. "What the fuck are you doing?" Scabius is still on his side, clutching his gut; Critter slides in front of him, blocking me. I guess he doesn't think I'd kick him too.

"What does it look like I'm doing?" I say, and sneer at him. "I'm waking him up," and scuttle sideways like I'm gonna kick again.

"Wait wait wait wait wait," Critter goes, and holds his hand up; he thinks I'm freaking out. He doesn't know I'm thinking clearer than them all. "Tracy, what's going on?" He says it in a dad voice, trying to sound all calm, but I can tell by his eyes he thinks I'm shit. He looks back at Scabius like he's handling me.

I pause; he thinks he's winning. Then I shrug at him. "You know what? Fuck you, Critter. Don't condescend to me." There's a half-empty Colt 45 bottle next to Squid's pack. I reach down, grab its neck, and break it on the brick. Leftover beer spills on my hand; it's cold. I shake it off.

I take a step toward them. Scabius has his breath back now and he gets up. Critter stands up too, staying close between us. It's funny: he's protecting Scabius from me. I watch them for a second, and I can see the whole thing: how they look out for each other, keep each other safe, so it can all keep on going along. Scabius can rape girls in alleys and Critter gets to hit them in the face, and nobody ever has to pay for any of it because when it all comes down they've got each other's back. Like someone's fucking parents. It's sick.

I look at Scabius. "You shit," I say, and then I spit on him again. "You're disgusting, you know that? I should rip apart your fucking face." I've got the bottle in my hand, cold and sharp, and I hold it up. He cowers. I can tell he wants to tear back into me but he knows he can't. He's too afraid I'll tell.

"God, you're such a pussy," I say. "Hiding behind big strong Critter, huh? Won't even come out from behind him." I laugh at him and look him up and down. I know that's what he hates the most: being treated like a girl. "You're just his bitch."

Then Critter gets up in my face. "Fuck you, Tracy," he says. His face is red. "He's my fucking *friend*. Which is something you obviously don't understand."

I snort at him.

"What?" Critter goes. "It's true. You've never had a friend in your life. All you do is use everyone and run off when you're done."

My grip on the bottle gets tighter and my eyes fill up at the corners. It stings; I blink and tears spill on my cheeks, itchy and hot. Critter sees and rips in harder. "We all see through your bullshit," he says. "You just take whatever you can get. You don't know what it means to care about someone. That's why you always leave." His face is smug, like he knows everything, like he's standing on high ground and he'll never get dirty or wet. "Scabius is my *friend*. That's better than you'll ever be."

"Yeah?" I say. I stop for a second and look at all of them. Squid and Rusty are still sitting down, watching. I can see the threads that tie the four of them together, like a spiderweb, sticky and thin and so much more fragile than any of them know. All the little assumptions that keep them from splitting up or crashing down, balanced on each other, teetering, and I know I'm about to pull the rug out, unravel all the threads. I give it one more second, watching how it all fits together: Squid's above-the-fray silence,

Rusty's quiet scared, Critter's big-daddy self-righteousness, and Scabius's fucking dirty lies. Then I pull it apart.

"He's your friend, huh?" I don't wait for an answer. "Well, guess what? Your friend threw your girlfriend up against a wall and raped her while you were off trying to score."

I just let it sit there. No one says anything. Squid and Rusty both hold their breath and look up at Scabius, I guess to see if it's true. Scabius looks like he did just after I kicked him, slouched down and caved in without any breath. Then he catches himself, stands up and squares his shoulders. "That's bullshit, man," he goes.

I fix my eyes on him. "It's bullshit?" I say. I stare him down. Tears are streaking down my cheeks but I don't care. "It never happened?" I want to kick the shit out of him, but I stay steady. "A block away from here, in the alley by El Centro, by the Dumpster in the afternoon, it never happened?"

I stay on him to make him answer. Everyone's eyes are on him now; Critter too. Finally he says "No," so soft you can hardly hear it, his eyes flickering around, pointed at the ground.

"You want to look at me and tell me that?" I ask, but I'm not asking. He doesn't say anything. "Or them, maybe," I say, nodding to the other guys. "Maybe you should tell them. Or maybe you should tell them how you did it to Eeyore too."

His eyes snap up at me and he starts stammering. "No

way, man," he goes, backing up. "I never did that." Everyone's staring at him. He looks at Critter. "I fucking promise, man," he goes. "I never did that. I never touched—"

By the look on Critter's face I can tell he knows that's not true. "You sure?" I interrupt Scabius. Nobody even asks how I know Eeyore; they just accept it. I don't have to explain myself. I feel like a cop. It feels good.

"Okay, well, fine, we hooked up, but that was because of her, man, she started it, you saw that"—he says to Critter, and Critter closes his eyes for a second to say yes— "but I never did what she's saying, we just hooked up, that was it, I swear."

"Why'd she leave, then, Scabius?" I ask him.

"What?" he goes, stalling. I roll my eyes. "I don't know, man, she left because—I don't fucking know! Ask her!"

"Yeah, well, I would, except she's busy turning tricks up near Toluca Lake, you fuck, because of whatever you did to her to make her leave."

Squid's already packing up his backpack, putting on Germ's leash; he's out. "That's fucked up, man," he says, but not loud enough to start a fight, and then he turns to Rusty. "Wanna go?" he asks him. Rusty looks like he's torn in half.

He turns up to me like he's asking permission. His hand is clutched around Squid's backpack strap, making sure he can't leave without him. I can tell he believes me, and I know he wants to stay and tell me that, or yell at Scabius, or talk to me, or something. But I can also tell that would mean admitting that he knew me before, back in Venice. It's obvious he's never told them that. And I guess I understand: telling them would mean explaining what he was doing over there, and I know he can't. And it's obvious he wants to be with Squid. So I just say "Go ahead." He sort of flinches, embarrassed that I could tell what he was asking without him even saying it, embarrassed that he's leaving. I won't tell him it's okay, because it's not. But I say "Go." And he looks at me for one more second, and then he gets up, and him and Squid leave with the dog.

Scabius watches them go, glad I'm paying attention to someone else, I'm sure. But it's dark so they're out of sight fast, and then there's nowhere to look but back at me.

He gets all hard, turning his face to a shell, but I can see it's sick and rotten underneath. I don't want to fucking talk to him anymore. I turn to Critter.

"You know what happened. Okay? I told you. So don't tell me how he's your fucking friend, and how he cares about you so much, and all that shit. He raped your fucking girlfriend. Not to mention your twelve-year-old friend or whatever who obviously worshipped you. And I don't see you doing anything about it. So don't tell me about using people and leaving them alone."

"She's lying, man," Scabius says. His eyes are jumping all over the place again. "You know she's fucking manipulative, man. Don't get sucked in."

I can't even say anything to that. I'm not going to argue

with him. I don't have to prove shit to Critter; if he wants to believe Scabius, there's nothing I can do. And all of a sudden the whole thing lifts off of me; the push drains from my veins and I feel light, like I'm filled with air instead. "Fuck you both," I say, and then I turn and walk away and leave them there, Scabius lying and Critter trying to decide whether to believe him, even though the truth is completely fucking obvious.

"Tracy," Critter calls after me when I'm halfway to the street. I don't turn around. I just keep walking toward the fluorescent light of the all-night donut shop, broken bottle still gripped tight in my hand.

I turn the corner sharp out of the alley. Blood rushes through my veins like wind; I didn't notice how hard my heart was beating. When I come up to Benito's, Bianca's still there, all pockmarks and purple lipstick, high-up tits and leopard print. This time she sees me before I can duck away. "Hey, *mami*," she goes, exactly like I knew she would, and I can't pretend not to hear her.

"Hey," I go, hoping that'll be the end of it.

"Where's your friend?" she asks me, and I think she must mean Critter. The whores all think he's cute.

"You can have him," I go. "He's a fucking asshole. Have fun."

"Damn, who's he and what'd he do to you?" She laughs and bites into her burrito. "No, I mean that little one, *mami*.

232

With the purple hair. Last time I saw you she was following you everywhere, and now you all alone. Where'd you put her?"

"I didn't put her fucking anywhere," I say. It comes out hard. "What the fuck do you care, anyway?"

"She was just always hanging on to you and those stinky-ass boys, that's all. And then I came back in town, she wasn't around no more. That's all I'm saying, damn."

"Yeah, well, maybe she had someplace she wanted to go," I say, and even as it comes out of my mouth I feel sick, not because I'm sober but because I know I'm lying. Eeyore didn't have anyplace she wanted to go. That's the whole fucking problem. The only place she wanted to be was with me, which I know because she told me, and I took off. I took off for Venice and I didn't take her with me. I told myself I didn't want to bring her into it, but really I just didn't want to be reminded of the shit she made me think about. She kept talking about staring at the ceiling and hands that break you open and he started showing up inside my dreams again, my fucking dad, and Ruthanne still stuck back in that bed, all soft skin and closed eyes, and it bubbled up until I couldn't stand it anymore. I had to go. I had to get away from the shit inside my head, my bedroom and the night sweats, and I didn't take her with me, I just left her there. And now I'm leaving her again.

I look down at the bottle, still in my hand; it's slippery with my sweat, wet against the hard cold, sharp at the edges.

233

I tuck it into the pocket of my hoodie, mouth end out, careful not to cut myself. "I gotta go," I say, not looking at Bianca. "See you later," even though I know I won't.

"Guess I won't look out for anyone no more," she goes. I walk away. "Yeah, fuck you too," she yells after me as I head east.

I get over to the 101 as quick as I can and stick my thumb out fast. I don't want to risk walking: on foot, you can always turn around. But once you slam the door and slouch down in the passenger side you can't get out. In a car you're a part of what's already moving, fixed in one direction, on your way to wherever the road dumps you. I get picked up by some guy in an Acura. He tries to talk to me. I look out the window and finger the glass in my pocket.

When he lets me off I don't even close the door behind me, I just run. Trying to keep up with the highway. I go at least ten blocks before I'm out of breath; by the time I slow down I'm too close to turn back. It's early still, probably six; the sun's barely up but the trucks are out, backed up to the warehouses, beeping. I'm sure Rob's still asleep.

I'm all ready to break in through the window but I try the door first and it's open. How stupid can you get? The hinges creak when I push it; steel scrapes against the concrete floor, but I go slow so they won't hear. Rob's got his mattress laid out between the door and Eeyore's corner, like he's guarding her or something. He's on his side, in his clothes still, drooling on the pillow. I'm just glad he's not in bed with her.

I tiptoe over to the corner. Eeyore's curled around her backpack, clutching it to her chest like a teddy bear. I watch her breathe for a minute, black-rimmed eyelids casting shadows on her sunken cheeks. That first morning I left, she looked like a baby: chubby face, bow mouth with the pin through it. Now she's a husk. I touch her hair. This time it wakes her up instead of putting her to sleep. Her eyes flutter open and she startles to see me; "Shh," I say, right before she talks. "Put your backpack on and be quiet," I whisper. "You're getting out of here."

"Where?" she says, still bleary.

I hadn't thought of that. "Somewhere better" is all I can come up with.

She rubs her eyes and wakes up more; then she looks over at Rob. "I don't know," she says.

"What do you mean, you don't know? I'm getting you out of here. Come on."

"But what about you," she whispers back. "Rob told me you need the drugs. You'll just come back without me later and keep everything for yourself."

I can't tell her it's not true. It probably is. But I just know I have to get her out. "It doesn't matter what I do," I say. "Come on. You shouldn't be here."

She looks at me for another second that stretches on

and on and on. Half of her is with me out the door; the other half's stuck in a habit, poured into a groove, curled up here with Rob. I can practically see the line traced down the middle of her. I know if I say anything it could push her either way. I just stare back at her. I don't look away.

Finally she whispers "Okay" and starts to lift herself up. My whole chest fills with relief.

I'm still crouched down, squatting, and she leans on my shoulder to stand. I lose my balance; the bottle drops out of my pocket and clinks on the concrete floor. I flinch. Rob's up right away.

He doesn't talk; just turns toward the noise and sees us. He can tell I didn't come back here to work. He looks at Eeyore's zipped-up backpack and the blankets thrown off, and heads right in our direction. Eeyore crouches down, knees tucked into her chest. I start to get up, moving slow so Rob won't pounce. I squat on my heels, one hand back toward Eeyore and the other held out in front of me like Critter when he was trying to calm me down. I smile. "It's cool, man," I say.

He doesn't care. "You're not taking her," he says.

I've had this hot feeling beneath the middle of my chest since Hollywood, right above the sick. Now it hammers like a heartbeat, hard enough to move my skin. I stop worrying about whether or not I'm going to turn around; I'm moving now, on a highway headed somewhere I can't stop. I swallow hard. "Fuck you I'm not," I say.

I've always kept up my end of the trade-off with Rob, known the rules and stayed inside them. With guys like him, as long as you do that you're pretty much safe, and as soon as you stop it they snap. Eeyore's foot moves away from my hand; I hear cloth scrape on concrete. I glance over my shoulder, see her huddled in the corner, as far away as she can get without running. I slide sideways in front of her, scoop the bottle up and slide it back into my pocket too fast for Rob to see.

He's right above me now, breath sour: I can smell it even from down on the floor. Sweat rides his forehead like a wave; his face reddens. Eeyore presses back against the wall. She's never seen him mad. I stand up, blocking him.

He pauses for a second, weighing whether to push me or tell me to move. I almost shove him to the side and run, but I stop: I don't know what he keeps in his pocket, and by the time I could grab Eeyore he might hurt both of us. I have to do something, though, or else he'll just push past me to Eeyore and that'll be it.

Before he can move I reach my hand down, slip my finger in his belt loop, pull him toward me. I hold him there, his zipper pressed against my stomach; I blink my eyes up at him slow, turn them into magnets, curl my lip into a smirk. I've done it so many times I can slip it on like clothes. It always works: they never see the sick beneath that face, or the nauseous, or the hate. All I have to do is slide my tongue across my teeth and they think it's the truth.

In my head I say to Eeyore, *Run*. I say it so loud it hurts inside my ears but she doesn't hear me, just stays stuck to the concrete wall, curled in around herself, too scared to move. I pull Rob closer, finger locked in his jeans, buying time; his eyes dart back and forth from me to Eeyore, speeding up, and then they fix on me. I can tell he half knows what I'm doing and it makes him mad, but he still likes it. I lick my lips. He gets that lost-animal look I know from Critter and so many other guys, when they can't tell whether to fuck you or hit you. Really they want both at once, but they think they have to choose. And the *hit her* wraps the *fuck her* like a rope, pulls tight enough to make their brains go red like tied-up flesh; they keep trying to untie that rope inside their heads when really all they want is it to pull until it cuts the circulation off. That's what that look is. You usually wind up getting the punch in the face.

He yanks away and hits me. For a second everything is black and sharp and wide and I almost fall backward, but my hand stays in my pocket on the glass.

I stagger forward, squinting through the spots in my eyes; when I get close enough I raise my arm and bring the bottle down across his cheek. It opens like a faucet. It's amazing how much faces bleed. He clutches his hand to the cut and blood pours through his fingers, soaking the floor. Now I say it out loud. *"Run,"* I yell at Eeyore. "Get the fuck out of here."

She's still standing there, holding on to her backpack like it's her only friend. "Are you coming?" she says. "I'm only going if you come with me."

I don't answer. I just grab her by the hand and drag her out.

Outside we run until we're winded, past beige houses and the minivans. The whole time I keep her hand in mine, tight around her little fingers, afraid of where I'll end up if I let go. When we cross the 101 and come up to Cahuenga she looks south toward Hollywood, all the places that we know. She slows down for a second, not knowing anyplace else to go, but I pull her arm and steer us past the turn and we keep moving east.

The roads start to slant up and curve, and we end up in those hills I always watch from the smog-cloaked highway, thick with palm trees and juniper, bougainvillea and figs. It's green here and we wind up through the hairpin streets, passing signs for roads I've never heard of, dodging too-big cars snapped fast around corners, stumbling to the curb just in time. Where the hills get really steep the houses stop: the ground's too sharp to build anything solid on, too rough to pour foundations, settle in. It's just wild, the way that it's supposed to be, snake vines strangling the cottonwoods, orange sand and gravel, broken glass. We turn off the street and scramble over wire fence and up the hill, tearing through the yucca like some kind of desert jungle, watching for poison ivy and burglar alarms, and the dust washes up on our jeans and turns us brown, and the hill's so steep it's almost like a mountain, and we climb, Eeyore and me, scraping our palms on the rocks and staying together.

When we get to the top we finally stop, panting, and the city spills out, water below us. The sun's hot enough to burn off the smog and you can see between the branches all the way to the ocean, mountains ringed around the city like a moat, cars pulsing through highways like blood. Eeyore's palm sweats into the lines in mine, and I can feel how soft the skin of her hand still is. I look at her; she doesn't notice. Still catching her breath, she's watching the canyon, her eyes little-kid wide at the hugeness of it.

"I used to come up here," she says. "Before Brian . . . moved in. My dad would bring me up here after school and teach me the names of all the flowers. We used to live right down"—she squints and points with her free hand—"there." I follow her finger down the other side of the hill to the house we broke into six months ago, white with a rust-colored roof, so close you can almost make out the doorway. "Or I mean, *I* used to. They still live there. I'm the only one that's gone."

The brand-new street-kid shell she's grown is still fragile as a robin's egg, too thin to hold the wet that's welling up behind it. When she breathes out it starts streaking down her face and then she doubles over, fast, like someone knocked the wind from her. Suddenly she's sobbing: tears hitting the orange dirt, turning it brown.

I crouch down next to her, breathe into her dirty purple hair. It's weird to see a person cry—I can't remember when the last time was—and even weirder to hold them while they do it. Her bones knock up against mine. She's tiny beneath her sweatshirt. I don't think I was ever that small.

After a minute the sobs slow down; she stops jerking in my arms so I don't have to hold on so tight. All of a sudden my hands feel sharp and clumsy on her little body. She looks up at me, eyes shot through with red, chest caved in with the kind of tired that's so huge you can't let yourself feel it or else you'll collapse. She's so tiny. And I see it: it's not just Rob she needs to get away from. She can't do this.

"You're going home," I tell her.

Her eyes flash fast and hot with fear, but there's something else behind them: a thing sort of like hope, or relief, or some other feeling I don't really know the name of. Blood floods my face. "Listen."

I make my eyes focused and straight, steady them on her. If I pause it'll open up a hole she could fall into, so I talk fast. "You have to tell. Here's what you do: you bring your dad up here and tell him what Brian did and that he has to make him leave. You just say it, just like that. Fuck Linda. Okay? Fuck Brian too. You don't have to be out here anymore. You can go back home. You have to. It's not safe out here for you."

She looks up at me like some kind of baby animal waiting to get fed. She's been hungry for too long, though; she's not sure there's food. She doesn't talk.

"It's hard out here, right?" I pick it back up, pull her along. I have to or she'll fall. "Really fucking hard." Her face answers yes. I nod. "Yeah. It's too hard for you. You're not like me; you don't belong out here."

It's funny: the tougher she fights, the younger she sounds. "You don't know what the fuck you're talking about. You don't know what's back there."

"Yes. I do." It comes out soft and still. "And there's a million Brians out here. Down there, there's only one."

She breaks my gaze and glues her eyeballs to the dust. Shakes her head. "I can't do it. I can't." Her chest hitches and her voice turns wet. "I can't go back. They're not gonna believe me." There's no question mark, but she's asking.

"How do you know that? Have you tried?" It comes out hard. As soon as it's out of my mouth I almost laugh—not like *I* tried. Not like I told. Not like I took my sister with me. I push it away. Eeyore's different.

"I already know! Squid and I broke in. Linda caught us and he told her. She said he was lying."

All of a sudden my breath goes shallow, panic flashes through. Maybe she's right. Maybe I'm wrong; maybe I'm lying and they won't believe her. Maybe I should have left her where at least she had a roof. The thought burrows like

242

a drill into my chest but I think *It's too late now*. I've brought her halfway; I can't leave her out here. And I can't let her go back there. If it's a lie I have to tell it. "But what about your dad? You never told him, right?" I say it with a question mark, but I'm not asking.

She opens her mouth to argue. I steel myself to fight back. It glints in my eyes, and when she sees it she folds in a flash. I'm so much harder than her, so much further down, and she is so, so tired. She breathes out and starts to cry again and shakes her head No. Now she's in my hands. I run with it.

"Okay, listen," I say, breathing in, making myself believe I'm pointing her the right way. Like hope, or faith or something, where you don't really know it's true but you reach for it anyway: you have to, just keep reaching out till your hands close around it. It's so long since I've believed anything I can hardly remember how. "You have to try. I mean it. If you don't, you're gonna die out here." That part I know.

"Come on." I make my voice as solid as I can and stand up, holding out my hand. She's clutching that backpack for dear life, face streaked, cheeks hot, eyes shining. Wind and traffic rustle through the bougainvillea. My lungs swell to hold the whole city, ten tons of purple smog, freeways reaching out like veins, like branches, like my hand stretching toward hers, waiting to see if she'll reach back and take it.

She does.

I pull her up, brush the dust from her jeans, wipe her face with the bottom of my tank top. I pry the backpack from her grip and put it on her shoulders. Then I hold them hard and look into her face.

"Can you do it?" The sun stretches out between us, hot, sticking our shirts to our skins and our skins to each other.

She nods. "Yeah," she says.

I wrap her hand in mine as we make our way down the other side of the hill, through the flowers she knows all the names of. "Tell me the names," I tell her. "It'll make you braver," and she does. Agave, jimsonweed, jacaranda. Hibiscus, matilija poppy, phlox. Remembering the things she knows. Laurel sumac. Sage. She names them all as we skid down the steep dirt, keep each other from falling, past the heaped-up dangling jade plants, through the cactus and the thorns.

When we get to the asphalt she leads the way.

Fifty yards from the green-painted doorway I stop and turn to her, sweat and blood streaking my cheeks, and then pull her in, press my lips to her forehead, smooth like mine might've been some time I can only almost remember. I want to keep her here, with me, but more than that I want to keep her safe, and I know that those are two separate places, as close and far apart from one another as this sidewalk and that house. I spin her around, turn her back to me and push her forward, and she walks, pulling the key out of her pocket, and when she puts it in the lock and cracks the door my sick gets swallowed up by something bigger, and this place I've never been before feels more like home than anything I've ever known.

Acknowledgments

Almost Home began as an entirely private pursuit, written bit by bit, in secret, between acting and playwriting jobs—simply because these kids took up residence in my head and heart and decided to stay. It could never have become an actual *book* without the help and support of many wonderful people.

I'd like to thank Margaret Cardillo, my fabulous editor, for taking a risk and helping bring these kids to life with such enormous enthusiasm, commitment, and skill; and Joe Veltre, my agent, for being thoroughly lovely to work with, and for guiding me through the process of getting my first novel out into the world with great insight, intelligence, and a reassuringly steady hand. Everyone at Hyperion has been a joy to work with; I am enormously grateful for all their expertise and support. I'd also like to thank several people who helped shepherd this book through various stages of its development: Greer Hendricks at Atria, for reading some of these stories in a very young form and doing me the enormous favor of helping them to find representation; Michelle Tessler, for believing in the stories early on and offering the invaluable suggestion that they should weave together into a novel; Les Plesko at UCLA, for bringing it into the present tense; Allison Heiny, for generously helping me to navigate the YA universe; and Sarah Self at Gersh, for seeing the possibilities in this story and helping it develop into whatever form it might take next.

Leslie Garis read the manuscript deeply and closely; her input and willingness to engage so fully were indispensable and inspiring. Natasha Blank—with her precocious intelligence and big heart—helped me stay true to these kids' young yet wise voices; April Yvette Thompson provided her customary unfailing barometer of emotional truth. Nick Hallett and Casey Kait, my two oldest closest artist friends, have shaped this book and all the other work I've made in ways far too many to count. I'm so grateful to have had their brilliant, specific, and hilarious sensibilities around to inform, intertwine with, and influence mine for the last almost-fifteen years. Jason Helm, my writing soulmate and emotional twin, has guided, grounded, expanded, developed, and deepened these characters, their stories, and each and every sentence that helps tell them. I never knew I could share a language with someone the way I do with him; my process and work wouldn't be what they are without his writing, his spirit, and his friendship.

I cannot say enough times how incredibly grateful I am to my parents, Art and Donna Blank. I feel so blessed to have been raised lovingly in a creative household by cool and interesting and conscious parents, and I owe the fact that I am even able to do things like write books in the first place largely to them. Thank you, Mom and Dad.

And finally, I want to thank my amazing husband, Erik Jensen. Making work with him taught me how to tell a story; living with him teaches me, every day, how to love. I am continually astonished that I get not only a hilarious, kind, inspiring best friend whom I'm madly in love with, but a brave, brilliant, and truth-telling artist who collaborates with me, supports me in my own work, is constantly spilling over with a gazillion ideas, and always helps me to do better. Thank you, Erik, for being my home.

Author's Note

The kids in *Almost Home* are fictional, but unfortunately, their situation isn't. More than 1.5 million teens in America run away each year—joined by at least a million "throwaways," kids who are kicked out or abandoned by their parents. Teens often wind up homeless after years of abuse, neglect, and/or family struggles with addiction; many bounce around in foster homes for years before winding up on the streets. And once they're out there, they are incredibly vulnerable. If you're homeless and a kid, it can be very difficult to do the things—like go to school and get a job—that will enable you to survive. Many homeless kids are too young to work a job legally, and often wind up being forced to sell drugs, or to exchange sex for food, clothes, or shelter.

Living on the streets is hard. Depression and post-traumatic stress disorder are three times as high among runaway youth; at least sixty percent of homeless kids are believed to be victims of serious physical or sexual abuse. Forty-one percent of teens on the street have been abandoned by their parents or guardians. Thirty-five to fifty percent of homeless youth identify as gay, lesbian, bisexual, or transgender; the vast majority of these kids have been kicked out of their homes just for being who they are.

There are dedicated people out there committed to helping homeless teens survive—but the problem is huge and resources are few. If this issue is something you care about, please consider volunteering at a shelter or drop-in center, or working to raise awareness about the struggles of homeless teens. Write to your representatives, or get active in your area.

And if you or someone you know is on the street or at risk, you're not alone. Below are some resources for teens on the street or in crisis:*

NATIONAL:

National Safe Place Program: Safe Place is a network of sites across America that provide immediate help and resources for all young people in crisis. To find a Safe Place in your area, go to **www.nationalsafeplace.org** or call 1-888-290-7233.

National Runaway Switchboard: Operates a 24-hour crisis line at 1-800-RUNAWAY. Call if you are thinking of running away, or if you have a friend who has run and needs help. NRS also runs the HOME FREE program with Greyhound Bus Lines, providing free bus rides home to runaway youth who want to get home.

Runaway Hotline: Runaway Hotline serves as a nationwide information and referral center for homeless youth needing food, shelter, medical assistance, counseling, and related services. 1-800-231-6946.

Covenant House: Provides shelter and services to homeless youth in more than fifteen cities nationwide, and operates the Nineline, 1-800-999-9999, a 24-hour crisis line for youth. The Nineline provides crisis counseling and referrals from a database of over 30,000 shelters and organizations helping teens. **www.covenanthouse.org**

Children's Rights of America: Offers support and crisis counseling for runaways and other youth. 1-800-442-HOPE.

OTHER RESOURCES:

Childhelp USA: A national, 24-hour toll-free hotline for child abuse. 1-800-4-A-CHILD.

The Trevor Project: A 24-hour hotline for gay, lesbian, bisexual, and transgender teens in crisis. 1-866-4-U-Trevor. **www.thetrevorproject.org**

Children of the Night: Twenty-four-hour help for teenage prostitutes or kids involved in pornography; rescue from pimps, shelter referrals, court appearances, medical appointments, tickets home, birth certificates, and other assistance. Twenty-four-hour hotline: 1-800-551-1300. **www.childrenofthenight.org**

Legal Services for Children: Provides confidential legal and related social services to young people free of charge. Help with guardianship, education, mental health, and foster care issues. 415-863-3762.

Roaddawgz: An educational and creative community by and for homeless youth, aimed at empowerment, mutual support, and community building. **www.roaddawgz.org**

*This list is meant to serve as a resource, and not as an endorsement. All organizations listed herein are solely responsible for their own conduct and actions.